Mary Wilder Tileston

Classic Heroic Ballads

Mary Wilder Tileston

Classic Heroic Ballads

ISBN/EAN: 9783744788366

Printed in Europe, USA, Canada, Australia, Japan

Cover: Foto ©Andreas Hilbeck / pixelio.de

More available books at **www.hansebooks.com**

CLASSIC HEROIC BALLADS.

The Classic Series.

Classic

Heroic Ballads

SELECTED BY THE

EDITOR OF "QUIET HOURS"

BOSTON

ROBERTS BROTHERS

1883

UNIVERSITY PRESS:
JOHN WILSON AND SON, CAMBRIDGE.

PREFACE.

My object in preparing this book has been to bring together from many sources the best and most stirring ballads of heroism and adventure, such as children — and, indeed, people of all ages — are always eager to hear. Such poetry fills an important place in a true education, by presenting a lofty ideal, and stimulating the heroic spirit. I have arranged the ballads in the chronological order of the events to which they relate, as nearly as was practicable.

I wish to express my thanks to Messrs. Houghton, Mifflin, & Co., and to Messrs. D. Appleton & Co., for the use of copyrighted poems, and also to the authors who have kindly allowed me to make this use of their poems.

M. W. T.

CONTENTS.

CONTENTS.

CLASSIC HEROIC BALLADS.

HORATIUS.

A LAY MADE ABOUT THE YEAR OF THE CITY CCCLX.

LARS PORSENA of Clusium
   By the Nine Gods he swore
That the great house of Tarquin
   Should suffer wrong no more.
By the Nine Gods he swore it,
   And named a trysting day,
And bade his messengers ride forth,
East and west and south and north,
   To summon his array.

East and west and south and north
   The messengers ride fast,
And tower and town and cottage
   Have heard the trumpet's blast.
Shame on the false Etruscan
   Who lingers in his home,
When Porsena of Clusium
   Is on the march for Rome.

The horsemen and the footmen
   Are pouring in amain,
From many a stately market-place ;
   From many a fruitful plain ;
From many a lonely hamlet,
   Which, hid by beech and pine,
Like an eagle's nest, hangs on the crest
   Of purple Apennine ;

From lordly Volaterræ,
   Where scowls the far-famed hold
Piled by the hands of giants
   For godlike kings of old ;
From seagirt Populonia,
   Whose sentinels descry
Sardinia's snowy mountain-tops
   Fringing the southern sky ;

From the proud mart of Pisæ,
   Queen of the western waves,
Where ride Massilia's triremes
   Heavy with fair-haired slaves ;
From where sweet Clanis wanders
   Through corn and vines and flowers ;
From where Cortona lifts to heaven
   Her diadem of towers.

Tall are the oaks whose acorns
    Drop in dark Auser's rill ;
Fat are the stags that champ the boughs
    Of the Ciminian hill ;
Beyond all streams Clitumnus
    Is to the herdsman dear ;
Best of all pools the fowler loves
    The great Volsinian mere.

But now no stroke of woodman
    Is heard by Auser's rill ;
No hunter tracks the stag's green path
    Up the Ciminian hill ;
Unwatched along Clitumnus
    Grazes the milk-white steer ;
Unharmed the water-fowl may dip
    In the Volsinian mere.

The harvests of Arretium
    This year, old men shall reap ;
This year, young boys in Umbro
    Shall plunge the struggling sheep ;
And in the vats of Luna,
    This year, the must shall foam
Round the white feet of laughing girls,
    Whose sires have marched to Rome.

There be thirty chosen prophets,
  The wisest of the land,
Who alway by Lars Porsena
  Both morn and evening stand :
Evening and morn the Thirty
  Have turned the verses o'er,
Traced from the right on linen white
  By mighty seers of yore.

And with one voice the Thirty
  Have their glad answer given :
" Go forth, go forth, Lars Porsena ;
  Go forth, beloved of Heaven ;
Go, and return in glory
  To Clusium's royal dome ;
And hang round Nurscia's altars
  The golden shields of Rome."

And now hath every city
  Sent up her tale of men ;
The foot are fourscore thousand,
  The horse are thousands ten.
Before the gates of Sutrium
  Is met the great array.
A proud man was Lars Porsena
  Upon the trysting day,

For all the Etruscan armies
   Were ranged beneath his eye,
And many a banished Roman,
   And many a stout ally;
And with a mighty following
   To join the muster came
The Tusculan Mamilius,
   Prince of the Latian name.

But by the yellow Tiber
   Was tumult and affright;
From all the spacious champaign
   To Rome men took their flight.
A mile around the city,
   The throng stopped up the ways;
A fearful sight it was to see,
   Through two long nights and days.

For aged folk on crutches,
   And women great with child,
And mothers sobbing over babes
   That clung to them and smiled,
And sick men borne in litters
   High on the necks of slaves,
And troops of sun-burned husbandmen
   With reaping-hooks and staves, —

And droves of mules and asses
　　Laden with skins of wine,
And endless flocks of goats and sheep,
　　And endless herds of kine,
And endless trains of wagons
　　That creaked beneath the weight
Of corn-sacks and of household goods,
　　Choked every roaring gate.

Now, from the rock Tarpeian,
　　Could the wan burghers spy
The line of blazing villages
　　Red in the midnight sky.
The Fathers of the City,
　　They sat all night and day,
For every hour some horseman came
　　With tidings of dismay.

To eastward and to westward
　　Have spread the Tuscan bands ;
Nor house, nor fence, nor dovecote
　　In Crustumerium stands.
Verbenna down to Ostia
　　Hath wasted all the plain ;
Astur hath stormed Janiculum,
　　And the stout guards are slain.

I wis, in all the Senate,
   There was no heart so bold,
But sore it ached, and fast it beat,
   When that ill news was told.
Forthwith up rose the Consul,
   Up rose the Fathers all;
In haste they girded up their gowns,
   And hied them to the wall.

They held a council standing
   Before the River-Gate;
Short time was there, ye well may guess,
   For musing or debate.
Out spake the Consul roundly:
   " The bridge must straight go down;
For, since Janiculum is lost,
   Naught else can save the town."

Just then a scout came flying,
   All wild with haste and fear:
" To arms ! to arms ! Sir Consul;
   Lars Porsena is here."
On the low hills to westward
   The Consul fixed his eye,
And saw the swarthy storm of dust
   Rise fast along the sky.

And nearer fast and nearer
   Doth the red whirlwind come ;
And louder still, and still more loud
From underneath that rolling cloud,
Is heard the trumpet's war-note proud,
   The trampling, and the hum.
And plainly and more plainly
   Now through the gloom appears,
Far to left and far to right,
In broken gleams of dark-blue light,
The long array of helmets bright,
   The long array of spears.

And plainly and more plainly,
   Above that glimmering line,
Now might ye see the banners
   Of twelve fair cities shine ;
But the banner of proud Clusium
   Was highest of them all,
The terror of the Umbrian,
   The terror of the Gaul.

And plainly and more plainly
   Now might the burghers know,
By port and vest, by horse and crest,
   Each warlike Lucomo.

There Cilnius of Arretium
    On his fleet roan was seen ;
And Astur of the fourfold shield,
Girt with the brand none else may wield ;
Tolumnius with the belt of gold ;
And dark Verbenna from the hold
    By reedy Thrasymene.

Fast by the royal standard,
    O'erlooking all the war,
Lars Porsena of Clusium
    Sat in his ivory car.
By the right wheel rode Mamilius,
    Prince of the Latian name ;
And by the left, false Sextus,
    That wrought the deed of shame.

But when the face of Sextus
    Was seen among the foes,
A yell that rent the firmament
    From all the town arose.
On the house-tops was no woman
    But spat towards him and hissed ;
No child but screamed out curses,
    And shook its little fist.

But the Consul's brow was sad,
    And the Consul's speech was low,
And darkly looked he at the wall,
    And darkly at the foe.
"Their van will be upon us
    Before the bridge goes down ;
And if they once may win the bridge,
    What hope to save the town ?"

Then out spake brave Horatius,
    The Captain of the Gate :
" To every man upon this earth
    Death cometh soon or late.
And how can man die better
    Than facing fearful odds,
For the ashes of his fathers
    And the temples of his Gods,

" And for the tender mother
    Who dandled him to rest,
And for the wife who nurses
    His baby at her breast,
And for the holy maidens
    Who feed the eternal flame,
To save them from false Sextus
    That wrought the deed of shame?

" Hew down the bridge, Sir Consul,
  With all the speed ye may ;
I, with two more to help me,
  Will hold the foe in play.
In yon strait path a thousand
  May well be stopped by three.
Now who will stand on either hand,
  And keep the bridge with me ? "

Then out spake Spurius Lartius ;
  A Ramnian proud was he :
" Lo, I will stand at thy right hand,
  And keep the bridge with thee."
And out spake strong Herminius ;
  Of Titian blood was he :
" I will abide on thy left side,
  And keep the bridge with thee."

" Horatius," quoth the Consul,
  " As thou sayest, so let it be."
And straight against that great array
  Forth went the dauntless Three.
For Romans in Rome's quarrel
  Spared neither land nor gold,
Nor son nor wife, nor limb nor life,
  In the brave days of old.

Then none was for a party;
    Then all were for the state;
Then the great man helped the poor,
    And the poor man loved the great;
Then lands were fairly portioned;
    Then spoils were fairly sold;
The Romans were like brothers
    In the brave days of old.

Now Roman is to Roman
    More hateful than a foe,
And the Tribunes beard the high,
    And the Fathers grind the low.
As we wax hot in faction,
    In battle we wax cold:
Wherefore men fight not as they fought
    In the brave days of old.

Now while the Three were tightening
    The harness on their backs,
The Consul was the foremost man
    To take in hand an axe;
And Fathers mixed with Commons
    Seized hatchet, bar, and crow,
And smote upon the planks above,
    And loosed the props below.

Meanwhile the Tuscan army,
    Right glorious to behold,
Came flashing back the noonday light,
Rank behind rank, like surges bright
    Of a broad sea of gold.
Four hundred trumpets sounded
    A peal of warlike glee,
As that great host, with measured tread,
And spears advanced, and ensigns spread,
Rolled slowly towards the bridge's head,
    Where stood the dauntless Three.

The Three stood calm and silent
    And looked upon the foes,
And a great shout of laughter
    From all the vanguard rose ;
And forth three chiefs came spurring
    Before that deep array ;
To earth they sprang, their swords they drew,
And lifted high their shields, and flew
    To win the narrow way ;

Aunus from green Tifernum,
    Lord of the Hill of Vines ;
And Seius, whose eight hundred slaves
    Sicken in Ilva's mines ;

And Picus, long to Clusium
   Vassal in peace and war,
Who led to fight his Umbrian powers
From that gray crag where, girt with towers,
The fortress of Nequinum lowers
   O'er the pale waves of Nar.

Stout Lartius hurled down Aunus
   Into the stream beneath;
Herminius struck at Seius,
   And clove him to the teeth;
At Picus brave Horatius
   Darted one fiery thrust;
And the proud Umbrian's gilded arms
   Clashed in the bloody dust.

Then Ocnus of Falerii
   Rushed on the Roman Three;
And Lausulus of Urgo,
   The rover of the sea;
And Aruns of Volsinium,
   Who slew the great wild boar,
The great wild boar that had his den
Amidst the reeds of Cosa's fen,
And wasted fields, and slaughtered men,
   Along Albinia's shore.

Herminius smote down Aruns ;
  Lartius laid Ocnus low ;
Right to the heart of Lausulus
  Horatius sent a blow.
" Lie there," he cried, " fell pirate !
  No more, aghast and pale,
From Ostia's walls the crowd shall mark
The track of thy destroying bark ;
No more Campania's hinds shall fly
To woods and caverns when they spy
  Thy thrice-accursèd sail."

But now no sound of laughter
  Was heard among the foes.
A wild and wrathful clamor
  From all the vanguard rose.
Six spears' length from the entrance
  Halted that deep array,
And for a space no man came forth
  To win the narrow way.

But hark ! the cry is *Astur ;*
  And lo ! the ranks divide ;
And the great Lord of Luna
  Comes with his stately stride.

Upon his ample shoulders
  Clangs loud the fourfold shield,
And in his hand he shakes the brand
  Which none but he can wield.

He smiled on those bold Romans
  A smile serene and high;
He eyed the flinching Tuscans,
  And scorn was in his eye.
Quoth he: "The she-wolf's litter
  Stand savagely at bay;
But will ye dare to follow
  If Astur clears the way?"

Then, whirling up his broadsword
  With both hands to the height,
He rushed against Horatius,
  And smote with all his might.
With shield and blade Horatius
  Right deftly turned the blow.
The blow, though turned, came yet too nigh;
It missed his helm, but gashed his thigh;
The Tuscans raised a joyful cry
  To see the red blood flow.

He reeled, and on Herminius
    He leaned one breathing-space ;
Then, like a wild-cat mad with wounds,
    Sprang right at Astur's face.
Through teeth, and skull, and helmet,
    So fierce a thrust he sped,
The good sword stood a hand-breadth out
    Behind the Tuscan's head.

And the great Lord of Luna
    Fell at that deadly stroke,
As falls on Mount Alvernus
    A thunder-smitten oak.
Far o'er the crashing forest
    The giant arms lie spread ;
And the pale augurs, muttering low,
    Gaze on the blasted head.

On Astur's throat Horatius
    Right firmly pressed his heel,
And thrice and four times tugged amain,
    Ere he wrenched out the steel.
" And see," he cried, " the welcome,
    Fair guests, that waits you here !
What noble Lucomo comes next,
    To taste our Roman cheer? "

But at his haughty challenge
   A sullen murmur ran,
Mingled of wrath, and shame, and dread,
   Along that glittering van.
There lacked not men of prowess,
   Nor men of lordly race ;
For all Etruria's noblest
   Were round the fatal place.

But all Etruria's noblest
   Felt their hearts sink to see
On the earth the bloody corpses,
   In the path the dauntless Three ;
And, from the ghastly entrance
   Where those bold Romans stood,
All shrank, like boys who unaware,
Ranging the woods to start a hare,
Come to the mouth of the dark lair
   Where, growling low, a fierce old bear
   Lies amidst bones and blood.

Was none who would be foremost
   To lead such dire attack ;
But those behind cried " Forward ! "
   And those before cried " Back ! "

And backward now and forward
   Wavers the deep array ;
And on the tossing sea of steel,
   To and fro the standards reel ;
And the victorious trumpet-peal
   Dies fitfully away.

Yet one man for one moment
   Strode out before the crowd ;
Well known was he to all the Three,
   And they gave him greeting loud.
" Now welcome, welcome, Sextus !
   Now welcome to thy home !
Why dost thou stay and turn away?
   Here lies the road to Rome."

Thrice looked he at the city ;
   Thrice looked he at the dead ;
And thrice came on in fury,
   And thrice turned back in dread ;
And, white with fear and hatred,
   Scowled at the narrow way
Where, wallowing in a pool of blood,
   The bravest Tuscans lay.

But meanwhile axe and lever
  Have manfully been plied,
And now the bridge hangs tottering
  Above the boiling tide.
" Come back, come back, Horatius ! "
  Loud cried the Fathers all ;
" Back, Lartius ! back, Herminius !
  Back, ere the ruin fall ! "

Back darted Spurius Lartius ;
  Herminius darted back ;
And, as they passed, beneath their feet
  They heard the timbers crack.
But when they turned their faces,
  And on the farther shore
Saw brave Horatius stand alone,
  They would have crossed once more.

But with a crash like thunder
  Fell every loosened beam,
And, like a dam, the mighty wreck
  Lay right athwart the stream ;
And a long shout of triumph
  Rose from the walls of Rome,
As to the highest turret-tops
  Was splashed the yellow foam.

And, like a horse unbroken
  When first he feels the rein,
The furious river struggled hard,
  And tossed his tawny mane,
And burst the curb, and bounded,
  Rejoicing to be free,
And whirling down, in fierce career,
Battlement, and plank, and pier,
  Rushed headlong to the sea.

Alone stood brave Horatius,
  But constant still in mind ;
Thrice thirty thousand foes before,
  And the broad flood behind.
" Down with him ! " cried false Sextus,
  With a smile on his pale face.
" Now yield thee," cried Lars Porsena,
  " Now yield thee to our grace."

Round turned he, as not deigning
  Those craven ranks to see ;
Naught spake he to Lars Porsena,
  To Sextus naught spake he ;
But he saw on Palatinus
  The white porch of his home ;
And he spake to the noble river
  That rolls by the towers of Rome.

"O Tiber! Father Tiber!
   To whom the Romans pray,
A Roman's life, a Roman's arms,
   Take thou in charge this day!"
So he spake, and speaking sheathèd
   The good sword by his side,
And with his harness on his back,
   Plunged headlong in the tide.

No sound of joy or sorrow
   Was heard from either bank;
But friends and foes in dumb surprise,
With parted lips and straining eyes,
   Stood gazing where he sank;
And when above the surges
   They saw his crest appear,
All Rome sent forth a rapturous cry,
And even the ranks of Tuscany
   Could scarce forbear to cheer.

But fiercely ran the current,
   Swollen high by months of rain;
And fast his blood was flowing;
   And he was sore in pain,

And heavy with his armor,
    And spent with changing blows ;
And oft they thought him sinking,
    But still again he rose.

Never, I ween, did swimmer,
    In such an evil case,
Struggle through such a raging flood
    Safe to the landing-place ;
But his limbs were borne up bravely
    By the brave heart within,
And our good Father Tiber
    Bare bravely up his chin.

" Curse on him ! " quoth false Sextus :
    " Will not the villain drown?
But for this stay, ere close of day
    We should have sacked the town ! "
" Heaven help him ! " quoth Lars Porsena,
    " And bring him safe to shore ;
For such a gallant feat of arms
    Was never seen before."

And now he feels the bottom ;
    Now on dry earth he stands ;

Now round him throng the Fathers
   To press his gory hands ;
And now, with shouts and clapping,
   And noise of weeping loud,
He enters through the River-Gate,
   Borne by the joyous crowd.

They gave him of the corn-land,
   That was of public right,
As much as two strong oxen
   Could plough from morn till night ;
And they made a molten image,
   And set it up on high,
And there it stands unto this day
   To witness if I lie.

It stands in the Comitium,
   Plain for all folk to see ;
Horatius in his harness,
   Halting upon one knee ;
And underneath is written,
   In letters all of gold,
How valiantly he kept the bridge
   In the brave days of old.

And still his name sounds stirring
   Unto the men of Rome,
As the trumpet-blast that cries to them
   To charge the Volscian home ;
And wives still pray to Juno
   For boys with hearts as bold
As his who kept the bridge so well
   In the brave days of old.

And in the nights of winter,
   When the cold north winds blow,
And the long howling of the wolves
   Is heard amidst the snow ;
When round the lonely cottage
   Roars loud the tempest's din,
And the good logs of Algidus
   Roar louder yet within ;

When the oldest cask is opened,
   And the largest lamp is lit ;
When the chestnuts glow in the embers,
   And the kid turns on the spit ;
When young and old in circle
   Around the firebrands close ;
When the girls are weaving baskets,
   And the lads are shaping bows ;

When the goodman mends his armor,
  And trims his helmet's plume ;
When the goodwife's shuttle merrily
  Goes flashing through the loom :
With weeping and with laughter
  Still is the story told,
How well Horatius kept the bridge
  In the brave days of old.

THOMAS BABINGTON MACAULAY.

ALFRED THE HARPER.

A.D. 878.

DARK fell the night, the watch was set,
    The host was idly spread,
The Danes around their watchfires met,
    Caroused, and fiercely fed.
They feasted all on English food,
    And quaffed the English ale ;
Their hearts leaped up with burning blood
    At each old Norseman tale.

The chiefs beneath a tent of leaves,
    And Guthrum, king of all,
Devoured the flesh of England's beeves,
    And laughed at England's fall.
Each warrior proud, each Danish earl,
    In mail and wolfskin clad,
Their bracelets white with plundered pearl,
    Their eyes with triumph mad.

A mace beside each king and lord
  Was seen, with blood bestained ;
From golden cups upon the board
  Their kindling wine they drained.
Ne'er left their sad, storm-beaten coast
  Sea-kings so hot for gore ;
'Mid Selwood's oaks so dreadful host
  Ne'er burnt a track before.

From Humber-land to Severn-land,
  And on to Tamar stream,
Where Thames makes green the towery strand,
  Where Medway's waters gleam, —
With hands of steel and mouths of flame
  They raged the kingdom through ;
And where the Norseman sickle came,
  No crop but hunger grew.

They loaded many an English horse
  With wealth of cities fair ;
They dragged from many a father's corse
  The daughter by her hair ;
And English slaves, and gems and gold,
  Were gathered round the feast ;
Till midnight in their woodland hold
  Oh ! never that riot ceased.

In stalked a warrior tall and rude
  Before the strong sea-kings ;
"Ye lords and earls of Odin's brood,
  Without a harper sings.
He seems.a simple man and poor,
  But well he sounds the lay,
And well, ye Norseman chiefs, be sure,
  Will ye the song repay."

In trod the bard with keen cold look,
  And glanced along the board,
That with the shout and war-cry shook,
  Of many a Danish lord.
But thirty brows, inflamed and stern,
  Soon bent on him their gaze,
While calm he gazed, as if to learn
  Who chief deserved his praise.

Lord Guthrum spake : " Nay, gaze not thus,
  Thou harper weak and poor !
By Thor ! who bandy looks with us,
  Must worse than looks endure.
Sing high the praise of Denmark's host,
  High praise each dauntless earl ;
The brave who stun this English coast
  With war's unceasing whirl."

The harper sat upon a block,
  Heaped up with wealthy spoil,
The wool of England's helpless flock,
  Whose blood had stained the soil.
He sat and slowly bent his head,
  And touched aloud the string ;
Then raised his face, and boldly said,
  " Hear thou my lay, O King !

" High praise from all whose gift is song
  To him in slaughter tried,
Whose pulses beat in battle strong,
  As if to meet his bride.
High praise from every mouth of man
  To all who boldly strive,
Who fall where first the fight began,
  And ne'er go back alive.

" But chief his fame be quick as fire,
  Be wide as is the sea,
Who dares in blood and pangs expire,
  To keep his country free.
To such, great earls, and mighty king !
  Shall praise in heaven belong ;
The starry harps their praise shall ring,
  And chime to mortal song.

" Fill high your cups, and swell the shout,
 At famous Regnar's name !
Who sank his host in bloody rout,
 When he to Humber came.
His men were chased, his sons were slain,
 And he was left alone.
They bound him in an iron chain
 Upon a dungeon stone.

" With iron links they bound him fast ;
 With snakes they filled the hole,
That made his flesh their long repast,
 And bit into his soul.
The brood with many a poisonous fang
 The warrior's heart beset ;
While still he cursed his foes, and sang
 His fierce, but hopeless threat.

" Great chiefs, why sink in gloom your eyes?
 Why champ your teeth in pain?
Still lives the song though Regnar dies !
 Fill high your cups again.
Ye too, perchance, O Norsemen lords !
 Who fought and swayed so long,
Shall soon but live in minstrel words,
 And owe your names to song.

"This land has graves by thousands more
　　Than that where Regnar lies.
When conquests fade, and rule is o'er,
　　The sod must close your eyes.
How soon, who knows? Not chief nor bard ;
　　And yet to me 't is given,
To see your foreheads deeply scarred
　　And guess the doom of Heaven.

"I may not read or when or how,
　　But earls and kings, be sure
I see a blade o'er every brow,
　　Where pride now sits secure.
Fill high the cups, raise loud the strain !
　　When chief and monarch fall,
Their names in song shall breathe again,
　　And thrill the feastful hall.

"Like God's own voice, in after years
　　Resounds the warrior's fame,
Whose deed his hopeless country cheers,
　　Who is its noblest name.
Drain down, O chiefs ! the gladdening bowl !
　　The present hour is yours ;
Let death to-morrow take the soul,
　　If joy to-day endures."

Grim sat the chiefs ; one heaved a groan,
   And one grew pale with dread ;
His iron mace was grasped by one,
   By one his wine was shed.
And Guthrum cried : " Nay, bard, no more
   We hear thy boding lay ;
Make drunk the song with spoil and gore ;
   Light up the joyous fray !

"Quick throbs my brain "— so burst the song —
   "To hear the strife once more.
The mace, the axe, they rest too long ;
   Earth cries, my thirst is sore.
More blithely twang the strings of bows
   Than strings of harps in glee ;
Red wounds are lovelier than the rose,
   Or rosy lips to me.

" Oh ! fairer than a field of flowers,
   When flowers in England grew,
Would be the battle's marshalled powers,
   The plain of carnage new.
With all its deaths before my soul
   The vision rises fair ;
Raise loud the song, and drain the bowl !
   I would that I were there !

" 'T is sweet to live in honored might,
    With true and fearless hand ;
'T is sweet to fall in freedom's fight,
    Nor shrink before the brand.
But sweeter far, when girt by foes,
    Unmoved to meet their frown,
And count with cheerful thought the woes
    That soon shall dash them down."

Loud rang the harp, the minstrel's eye
    Rolled fiercely round the throng ;
It seemed two crashing hosts were nigh,
    Whose shock aroused the song.
A golden cup King Guthrum gave
    To him who strongly played ;
And said, " I won it from the slave
    Who once o'er England swayed."

King Guthrum cried : " ' T was Alfred's own ;
    Thy song befits the brave ;
The king who cannot guard his throne
    Nor wine nor song shall have."
The minstrel took the goblet bright,
    And said : " I drink the wine
To him who owns by justest right
    The cup thou bidst be mine.

" To him, your lord, oh shout ye all !
 His meed be deathless praise !
The king who dares not nobly fall,
 Dies basely all his days.
The king who dares not guard his throne,
 May curses heap his head ;
But hope and strength be all his own,
 Whose blood is bravely shed."

" The praise thou speakest," Guthrum said,
 " With sweetness fills mine ear ;
For Alfred swift before me fled,
 And left me monarch here.
The royal coward never dared
 Beneath mine eye to stand.
Oh, would that now this feast he shared,
 And saw me rule his land ! "

Then stern the minstrel rose, and spake,
 And gazed upon the king :
" Not now the golden cup I take,
 Nor more to thee I sing.
Another day, a happier hour,
 Shall bring me here again ;
The cup shall stay in Guthrum's power
 Till I demand it then."

The harper turned and left the shed,
  Nor bent to Guthrum's crown :
And one who marked his visage said
  It wore a ghastly frown.
The Danes ne'er saw that harper more,
  For, soon as morning rose,
Upon their camp King Alfred bore,
  And slew ten thousand foes.

JOHN STERLING.

GARCI PEREZ DE VARGAS.

ABOUT 1248.

KING FERDINAND alone did stand one day upon the
    hill,
Surveying all his leaguer, and the ramparts of
    Seville ;
The sight was grand, when Ferdinand by proud
    Seville was lying,
O'er tower and tree far off to see the Christian
    banners flying.

Down chanced the king his eye to fling, where far
    the camp below,
Two gentlemen along the glen were riding soft and
    slow ;
As void of fear each cavalier seemed to be riding
    there,
As some strong hound may pace around the roe-
    buck's thicket lair.

It was Don Garci Perez, and he would breathe the
    air,
And he had ta'en a knight with him, that as lief had
    been elsewhere ;
For soon the knight to Garci said : " Ride, ride we,
    or we 're lost !
I see the glance of helm and lance — it is the
    Moorish host ! "

The Lord of Vargas turned him round, his trusty
    squire was near —
The helmet on his brow he bound, his gauntlet
    grasped the spear ;
With that upon his saddle-tree he planted him right
    steady —
" Now come," quoth he, " whoe'er they be, I trow
    they 'll find us ready."

By this the knight who rode with him had turned
    his horse's head,
And up the glen in fearful trim unto the camp had
    fled.
" Ha ! gone ? " quoth Garci Perez ; he smiled,
    and said no more,
But slowly, with his esquire, rode as he rode
    before.

It was the Count Lorenzo, just then it happened
    so,
He took his stand by Ferdinand, and with him
    gazed below ;
" My liege," quoth he, " seven Moors I see a-com-
    ing from the wood,
Now bring they all the blows they may, I trow
    they 'll find as good ;
But it is Don Garci Perez — if his cognizance they
    know,
I guess it will be little pain to give them blow for
    blow."

The Moors from forth the greenwood came riding
    one by one,
A gallant troop with armor resplendent in the
    sun ;
Full haughty was their bearing, as o'er the sward
    they came,
While the calm Lord of Vargas, his march was still
    the same.

They stood drawn up in order, while past them all
    rode he ;
For when upon his shield they saw the Red Cross
    and the Tree,

And the wings of the Black Eagle, that o'er his
    crest were spread
They knew Don Garci Perez, and never a word they
    said.

He took the casque from off his head, and gave it
    to the squire :
"My friend," quoth he, "no need I see why I my
    brows should tire."
But as he doffed the helmet, he saw his scarf was
    gone, —
"I 've dropped it sure," quoth Garci, "when I put
    my helmet on."

He looked around and saw the scarf, for still the
    Moors were near,
And they had picked it from the sward, and looped
    it on a spear.
"These Moors," quoth Garci Perez, " uncourteous
    Moors they be —
Now, by my soul, the scarf they stole, yet durst not
    question me !

"Now reach once more my helmet."   The esquire
    said him nay, —

" For a silken string why should ye fling perchance
  your life away ? "
" I had it from my lady," quoth Garci, " long ago,
And never Moor that scarf, be sure, in proud Seville
  shall show."

But when the Moslem saw him they stood in firm
  array ;
He rode among the armed throng, he rode right
  furiously.
" Stand, stand, ye thieves and robbers, lay down
  my lady's pledge ! "
He cried : — and ever as he cried they felt his
  falchion's edge.

That day the Lord of Vargas came to the camp
  alone ;
The scarf, his lady's largess, around his breast was
  thrown ;
Bare was his head, his sword was red, and from his
  pommel strung,
Seven turbans green, sore hacked I ween, before
  Don Garci hung.

J. G. LOCKHART.

Translated from the Spanish.

SIR PATRICK SPENS.

THE king sits in Dunfermline town,
  Drinking the blude-red wine :
" O where will I get a skeely skipper
  To sail this new ship of mine ? "

O up and spake an eldern knight,
  Sat at the king's right knee :
" Sir Patrick Spens is the best sailor
  That ever sailed the sea."

Our king has written a braid letter,
  And sealed it with his hand,
And sent it to Sir Patrick Spens,
  Was walking on the strand.

" To Noroway, to Noroway,
  To Noroway o'er the faem ;
The king's daughter of Noroway,
  'T is thou maun bring her hame ! "

The first word that Sir Patrick read,
　　Sae loud loud laughed he;
The neist word that Sir Patrick read
　　The tear blindit his e'e.

" O wha is this has done this deed,
　　And tauld the king o' me,
To send us out at this time o' the year,
　　To sail upon the sea?

" Be it wind, be it weet, be it hail, be it sleet,
　　Our ship must sail the faem;
The king's daughter of Noroway,
　　'T is we must fetch her hame."

They hoysed their sails on Monenday morn
　　Wi' a' the speed they may;
They hae landed in Noroway
　　Upon a Wodensday.

They hadna been a week, a week
　　In Noroway, but twae,
When that the lords o' Noroway
　　Began aloud to say:

" Ye Scottishmen spend a' our king's gowd
　　And a' our queenis' fee." —
" Ye lie, ye lie, ye liars loud!
　　Fu' loud I hear ye lie!

" For I hae brought as much white monie
  As gane [1] my men and me ;
And I hae brought a half-fou [2] of gude red gowd
  Out owre the sea wi' me.

" Make ready, make ready, my merry men a' !
  Our gude ship sails the morn." —
" Now, ever alake ! my master dear,
  I fear a deadly storm.

" I saw the new moon, late yestreen,
  Wi' the auld moon in her arm ;
And if we gang to sea, master,
  I fear we 'll come to harm."

They hadna sailed a league, a league,
  A league, but barely three,
When the lift [3] grew dark, and the wind blew loud,
  And gurly [4] grew the sea.

The ankers brak, and the topmasts lap,
  It was sic a deadly storm ;
And the waves came o'er the broken ship
  Till a' her sides were torn.

---

[1] *Gane,* — sufficed.   [2] *Half-fou,* — half-bushel.
[3] Sky.   [4] Rough, surly.

" O where will I get a gude sailor
   To take my helm in hand,
Till I get up to the tall topmast
   To see if I can spy land?"

" O here am I, a sailor gude,
   To take the helm in hand,
Till you go up to the tall topmast —
   But I fear you 'll ne'er spy land."

He hadna gane a step, a step,
   A step, but barely ane,
When a boult flew out of our goodly ship,
   And the salt sea it came in.

" Gae fetch a web o' the silken claith,
   Another o' the twine,
And wap them into our ship's side,
   And letna the sea come in."

They fetched a web o' the silken claith,
   Another o' the twine,
And they wapped them roun' that gude ship's
     side ;
   But still the sea came in.

O laith, laith were our good Scots lords
   To weet their cork-heeled shoon,
But lang or a' the play was played
   They wat their hats aboon !

And mony was the feather bed
  That fluttered on the faem ;
And mony was the gude lord's son
  That never mair came hame !

The ladyes wrang their fingers white —
  The maidens tore their hair ;
A' for the sake of their true loves —
  For them they 'll see na mair.

O lang lang may the ladyes sit,
  Wi' their fans into their hand,
Before they see Sir Patrick Spens
  Come sailing to the strand !

And lang lang may the maidens sit,
  Wi' their gowd kaims in their hair,
A' waiting for their ain dear loves —
  For them they 'll see na mair !

O forty miles off Aberdeen
  'T is fifty fathoms deep,
And there lies gude Sir Patrick Spens
  Wi' the Scots lords at his feet !

<small>SCOTT'S MINSTRELSY OF THE SCOTTISH BORDER.</small>

BANNOCKBURN:

ROBERT BRUCE'S ADDRESS TO HIS ARMY.

1314.

Scots, wha hae wi' Wallace bled,
Scots, wham Bruce has aften led ;
Welcome to your gory bed,
  Or to glorious victorie.

Now 's the day, and now 's the hour,
See the front o' battle lour ;
See approach proud Edward's power —
  Edward ! chains and slaverie.

Wha will be a traitor knave ?
Wha can fill a coward's grave ?
Wha sae base as be a slave ?
  Traitor ! coward ! turn and flee.

Wha for Scotland's king and law
Freedom's sword will strongly draw,
Freeman stand or freeman fa' ;
  Caledonian ! on wi' me !

By oppression's woes and pains !
By your sons in servile chains,
 We will drain our dearest veins,
     But they shall, — they shall be free !

Lay the proud usurpers low !
Tyrants fall in every foe !
Liberty 's in every blow !
     Forward ! let us do, or die !

ROBERT BURNS.

THE LORD OF BUTRAGO.

1385.

THE incident to which the following ballad relates is supposed to have occurred on the famous field of Aljubarrota, where King Juan the First, of Castile was defeated by the Portuguese. The King, who was at the time in a feeble state of health, exposed himself very much during the action ; and being wounded, had great difficulty in making his escape.

"YOUR horse is faint, my King — my Lord ! your
    gallant horse is sick —
His limbs are torn, his breast is gored, on his eye
    the film is thick ;
Mount, mount on mine, oh, mount apace, I pray
    thee, mount and fly !
Or in my arms I 'll lift your grace — these trampling
    hoofs are nigh !

"My King — my King ! you 're wounded sore —
    the blood runs from your feet ;
But only lay a hand before, and I 'll lift you to
    your seat :
Mount, Juan, for they gather fast ! — I hear their
    coming cry ;
Mount, mount, and ride for jeopardy — I 'll save
    you though I die !

"Stand, noble steed ! this hour of need — be gentle as a lamb :
I 'll kiss the foam from off thy mouth, thy master
   dear I am.
Mount, Juan, mount: whate'er betide, away the
   bridle fling,
And plunge the rowels in his side. My horse shall
   save my king !

"Nay, never speak ; my sires, Lord King, received
   their land from yours,
And joyfully their blood shall spring, so be it thine
   secures ;
If I should fly, and thou, my King, be found among
   the dead,
How could I stand 'mong gentlemen, such scorn
   on my gray head?

"Castile's proud dames shall never point the finger
   of disdain,
And say there 's ONE that ran away when our good
   lords were slain !
I leave Diego in your care — you 'll fill his father's
   place :
Strike, strike the spur, and never spare — God's
   blessing on your grace !"

So spake the brave Montañez, Butrago's Lord was
    he,
And turned him to the coming host in steadfastness
    and glee.
He flung himself among them, as they came down
    the hill ;
He died, God wot ! but not before his sword had
    drunk its fill.

J. G. LOCKHART.

Translated from the Spanish.

THE BATTLE OF OTTERBOURNE.

AUGUST 15, 1388.

It fell about the Lammas tide,
   When the muir-men win their hay,
The doughty Douglas bound him to ride
   Into England to drive a prey.

He chose the Gordons, and the Græmes,
   With them the Lindesays, light and gay ;
But the Jardines would not with him ride,
   And they rue it to this day.

And he has burned the dales of Tyne,
   And part of Bambrough shire ;
And three good towers on Reidswire fells,[1]
   He left them all on fire.

And he marched up to Newcastle,
   And rode it round about ;
"O, wha's the lord of this castle,
   Or wha's the lady o 't ? " —

[1] *Fells*, — hills, moors.

But up spake proud Lord Percy, then,
    And oh but he spake high !
" I am the lord of this castle,
    My wife 's the lady gay." —

" If thou 'rt the lord of this castle,
    Sae weel it pleases me !
For, ere I cross the Border fells,
    The tane of us shall die." —

He took a lang spear in his hand,
    Shod with the metal free,
And for to meet the Douglas there,
    He rode right furiouslie.

But oh how pale his lady looked,
    Frae aff the castle wa',
When down before the Scottish spear
    She saw proud Percy fa'.

" Had we twa been upon the green,
    And never an eye to see,
I wad hae had you, flesh and fell,[1]
    But your sword shall gae wi' me. —

---

[1] *Fell*, — hide. Douglas insinuates that Percy was rescued by his soldiers.

" But gae ye up to Otterbourne,
    And wait there dayis three ;
And if I come not ere three dayis end,
    A fause knight ca' ye me." —

" The Otterbourne 's a bonnie burn ;
    'T is pleasant there to be ;
But there is nought at Otterbourne,
    To feed my men and me.

" The deer rins wild on hill and dale,
    The birds fly wild from tree to tree ;
But there is neither bread nor kale,
    To fend[1] my men and me.

" Yet I will stay at Otterbourne,
    Where you shall welcome be ;
And, if ye come not at three dayis end,
    A fause lord I 'll ca' thee." —

" Thither will I come," proud Percy said,
    " By the might of Our Ladye ! "
" There will I bide thee," said the Douglas,
    " My troth I plight to thee."   .

---

[1] *Fend,* — support.

They lighted high on Otterbourne,
    Upon the bent [1] sae brown ;
They lighted high on Otterbourne,
    And threw their pallions [2] down.

And he that had a bonnie boy,
    Sent out his horse to grass ;
And he that had not a bonnie boy,
    His ain servant he was.

But up then spake a little page,
    Before the peep of dawn —
" O waken ye, waken ye, my good lord,
    For Percy 's hard at hand." —

" Ye lie, ye lie, ye liar loud !
    Sae loud I hear ye lie :
For Percy had not men yestreen
    To dight my men and me.

" But I have dreamed a dreary dream,
    Beyond the Isle of Sky ;
I saw a dead man win a fight,
    And I think that man was I."

[1] *Bent,* — field.
[2] Pavilions, tents.

He belted on his guid broad sword,
    And to the field he ran ;
But he forgot the helmet good,
    That should have kept his brain.

When Percy wi' the Douglas met,
    I wot he was fu' fain. [1]
They swapped [2] their swords, till sair they swat,
    And the blood ran down like rain.

But Percy with his good broad sword,
    That could so sharply wound,
Has wounded Douglas on the brow,
    Till he fell to the ground.

Then he called on his little foot-page,
    And said — " Run speedilie,
And fetch my ain dear sister's son,
    Sir Hugh Montgomery."

" My nephew good," the Douglas said,
    " What recks the death of ane !
Last night I dreamed a dreary dream,
    And I ken the day 's thy ain.

[1] *Fain,* — glad.
[2] *Swapped,* — struck violently.

" My wound is deep ; I fain would sleep ;
    Take thou the vanguard of the three,
And hide me by the bracken [1] bush,
    That grows on yonder lily lee.[2]

" O bury me by the bracken bush,
    Beneath the blooming brier,
Let never living mortal ken,
    That e'er a kindly Scot lies here."

He lifted up that noble lord,
    Wi' the saut tear in his e'e ;
He hid him in the bracken bush,
    That his merrie-men might not see.

The moon was clear, the day drew near,
    The spears in flinders flew,
But mony a gallant Englishman
    Ere day the Scotsmen slew.

The Gordons good, in English blood,
    They steeped their hose and shoon ;
The Lindsays flew like fire about,
    Till all the fray was done.

---

[1] *Bracken,* —fern.
[2] *Lee,* — field.

The Percy and Montgomery met,
  That either of other were fain ;
They swapped swords, and they twa swat,
  And aye the blood ran down between.

" Now yield thee, yield thee, Percy," he said,
  " Or else I vow I 'll lay thee low ! "
"To whom must I yield," quoth Lord Percy,
  " Now that I see it must be so ? "

" Thou shalt not yield to lord nor loon,
  Nor yet shalt thou yield to me ;
But yield thee to the bracken bush,
  That grows upon yon lily lee ! "

" I will not yield to a bracken bush,
  Nor yet will I yield to a brier ;
But I would yield to Earl Douglas,
  Or Sir Hugh the Montgomery, if he were here."

As soon as he knew it was Sir Hugh,
  He struck his sword's point in the ground ;
The Montgomery was a courteous knight,
  And quickly took him by the hand.

This deed was done at the Otterbourne
  About the breaking of the day ;
Earl Douglas was buried at the bracken bush,
  And the Percy led captive away.

Scott's Minstrelsy of the Scottish Border.

CHEVY-CHACE.

FOURTEENTH CENTURY.

God prosper long our noble king,
    Our lives and safeties all ;
A woeful hunting once there did
    In Chevy-Chace befall.

To drive the deer with hound and horn,
    Earl Percy took his way ;
The child may rue that is unborn,
    The hunting of that day.

The stout Earl of Northumberland
    A vow to God did make,
His pleasure in the Scottish woods
    Three summer days to take ;

The chiefest harts in Chevy-Chace
    To kill and bear away :
These tidings to Earl Douglas came,
    In Scotland where he lay :

Who sent Earl Percy present word,
   He would prevent his sport ;
The English Earl, not fearing that,
   Did to the woods resort,

With fifteen hundred bowmen bold ;
   All chosen men of might,
Who knew full well in time of need
   To aim their shafts aright.

The gallant greyhounds swiftly ran,
   To chase the fallow deer :
On Monday they began to hunt,
   When daylight did appear ;

And long before high noon they had
   A hundred fat bucks slain ;
Then having dined, the drovers went
   To rouse the deer again.

The bowmen mustered on the hills,
   Well able to endure ;
And all their rear, with special care,
   That day was guarded sure.

The hounds ran swiftly through the woods,
   The nimble deer to take,
That with their cries the hills and dales
   An echo shrill did make.

Lord Percy to the quarry went,
    To view the slaughtered deer;
Quoth he, " Earl Douglas promised
    This day to meet me here:

" But if I thought he would not come,
    No longer would I stay."
With that, a brave young gentleman
    Thus to the Earl did say:

" Lo, yonder doth Earl Douglas come,
    His men in armor bright:
Full twenty hundred Scottish spears
    All marching in our sight;

" All men of pleasant Tividale,
    Fast by the river Tweed;"
" Then cease your sports," Earl Percy said,
    " And take your bows with speed:

" And now with me, my countrymen,
    Your courage forth advance;
For never was there champion yet,
    In Scotland or in France,

" That ever did on horseback come,
    But if my hap it were,
I durst encounter man for man,
    With him to break a spear."

Earl Douglas on his milk-white steed,
　　Most like a baron bold,
Rode foremost of his company,
　　Whose armor shone like gold.

" Show me," said he, " whose men you be,
　　That hunt so boldly here,
That, without my consent, do chase
　　And kill my fallow deer."

The first man that did answer make,
　　Was noble Percy he ;
Who said, " We list not to declare,
　　Nor show whose men we be ;

" Yet will we spend our dearest blood,
　　Thy chiefest harts to slay."
Then Douglas swore a solemn oath,
　　And thus in rage did say, —

" Ere thus I will out-bravèd be
　　One of us two shall die :
I know thee well, an earl thou art ;
　　Lord Percy, so am I.

"But trust me, Percy, pity it were,
　　And great offence to kill
Any of these our guiltless men,
　　For they have done no ill.

" Let thou and I the battle try,
 And set our men aside."
" Accurst be he," Earl Percy said,
 " By whom this is denied."

Then stept a gallant squire forth,
 (Witherington was his name),
Who said, " I would not have it told
 To Henry, our king, for shame,

" That ere my captain fought on foot,
 And I stood looking on ;
You two be earls," quo' Witherington,
 " And I a squire alone ;

" I 'll do the best that do I may,
 While I have power to stand ;
While I have power to wield my sword,
 I 'll fight with heart and hand."

Our English archers bent their bows,
 Their hearts were good and true ;
At the first flight of arrows sent,
 Full fourscore Scots they slew.

Yet bides Earl Douglas on the bent,
 As chieftain stout and good ;
As valiant captain, all unmoved
 The shock he firmly stood.

His host he parted had in three,
   As leader ware and try'd ;
And soon his spearmen on their foes
   Bare down on every side.

Throughout the English archery
   They dealt full many a wound :
But still our valiant Englishmen
   All firmly kept their ground :

And throwing strait their bows away,
   They grasped their swords so bright ;
And now sharp blows, a heavy shower,
   On shields and helmets light.

They closed full fast on every side,
   No slackness there was found ;
And many a gallant gentleman
   Lay gasping on the ground.

O Christ ! it was a grief to see,
   How each one chose his share,
And how the blood out of their breasts
   Did gush like water clear.

At last these two stout earls did meet,
   Like captains of great might ;
Like lions wode,[1] they layd on lode,
   And made a cruel fight :

[1] *Wode*, — mad, furious.

They fought until they both did sweat,
   With swords of tempered steel;
Until the blood, like drops of rain,
   They trickling down did feel.

"Yield thee, Lord Percy," Douglas said;
   "In faith I will thee bring
Where thou shalt high advancèd be
   By James, our Scottish King;

"Thy ransom I will freely give,
   And this report of thee,
Thou art the most courageous knight,
   That ever I did see."

"No, Douglas," quoth Earl Percy then,
   "Thy proffer I do scorn;
I will not yield to any Scot
   That ever yet was born."

With that, there came an arrow keen
   Out of an English bow,
Which struck Earl Douglas to the heart,
   A deep and deadly blow;

Who never spake more words than these,
   "Fight on, my merry men all;
For why, my life is at an end,
   Lord Percy sees my fall."

Then leaving life, Earl Percy took
  The dead man by the hand ;
And said, " Earl Douglas, for thy life
  Would I had lost my land.

"O Christ ! my very heart doth bleed
  With sorrow for thy sake ;
For sure, a more redoubted knight
  Mischance did never take."

A knight amongst the Scots there was,
  Which saw Earl Douglas die,
Who straight in wrath did vow revenge
  Upon the Earl Percy :

Sir Hugh Montgomery was he called,
  Who, with a spear full bright,
Well mounted on a gallant steed,
  Ran fiercely through the fight ;

And past the English archers all,
  Without a dread or fear ;
And through Earl Percy's body then
  He thrust his hateful spear ;

With such vehement force and might
  He did his body gore,
The staff ran through the other side
  A large cloth-yard, and more.

So thus did both these nobles die,
   Whose courage none could stain ;
An English archer then perceived
   The noble earl was slain ;

He had a bow bent in his hand,
   Made of a trusty tree ;
An arrow of a cloth-yard long
   To the hard head haled he :

Against Sir Hugh Montgomery
   So right the shaft he set,
The gray goose-wing that was thereon
   In his heart's blood was wet.

This fight did last from break of day,
   Till setting of the sun ;
For when they rung the evening-bell,
   The battle scarce was done.

With stout Earl Percy, there was slain
   Sir John of Egerton,
Sir Robert Ratcliff, and Sir John,
   Sir James, that bold baron.

And with Sir George and stout Sir James,
   Both knights of good account,
Good Sir Ralph Raby there was slain,
   Whose prowess did surmount.

For Witherington my heart is woe,
    That ever he slain should be ;
For when his legs were hewn in two
    He knelt and fought on his knee.

And with Earl Douglas, there was slain
    Sir Hugh Montgomery,
Sir Charles Murray, that from the field
    One foot would never flee.

Sir Charles Murray of Ratcliff, too,
    His sister's son was he ;
Sir David Lamb, so well esteemed,
    But saved he could not be.

And the Lord Maxwell in like case
    Did with Earl Douglas die :
Of twenty hundred Scottish spears,
    Scarce fifty-five did fly.

Of fifteen hundred Englishmen,
    Went home but fifty-three ;
The rest in Chevy-Chace were slain,
    Under the green-wood tree.

Next day did many widows come,
    Their husbands to bewail ;
They washed their wounds in brinish tears,
    But all would not prevail.

Their bodies, bathed in purple blood,
   They bore with them away :
They kissed them dead a thousand times,
   Ere they were clad in clay.

The news was brought to Eddenborrow,
   Where Scotland's king did reign,
That brave Earl Douglas suddenly
   Was with an arrow slain :

"O heavy news," King James did say,
   "Scotland can witness be,
I have not any captain more,
   Of such account as he."

Like tidings to King Henry came,
   Within as short a space,
That Percy of Northumberland
   Was slain in Chevy-Chace :

"Now God be with him," said our king,
   "Sith 't will no better be ;
I trust I have, within my realm,
   Five hundred as good as he ;

"Yet shall not Scot nor Scotland say,
   But I will vengeance take ;
I 'll be revengèd on them all,
   For brave Earl Percy's sake."

This vow full well the king performed
　　After, at Humbledown ;
In one day fifty knights were slain,
　　With lords of high renown :

And of the rest, of small account,
　　Did many hundreds die.
Thus endeth the hunting of Chevy-Chace,
　　Made by the Earl Percy.

God save the king, and bless this land
　　With plenty, joy, and peace ;
And grant, henceforth, that foul debate
　　'Twixt noblemen may cease.

BATTLE OF HARLAW.

1411.

Now haud your tongue, baith wife and carle,
    And listen great and sma',
And I will sing of Glenallan's earl
    That fought on the red Harlaw.

The coronach 's cried on Bennachie,
    And down the Don and a',
And hieland and lawland may mournfu' be
    For the sair field of Harlaw.

They saddled a hundred milk-white steeds,
    They hae bridled a hundred black,
With a chafron of steel on each horse's head,
    And a good knight upon his back.

They hadna ridden a mile, a mile,
    A mile but barely ten,
When Donald came branking down the brae
    Wi' twenty thousand men.

Their tartans they were waving wide,
   Their glaives were glancing clear,
The pibrochs rung frae side to side,
   Would deafen you to hear.

The great Earl in his stirrups stood,
   That Highland host to see :
" Now here 's a knight that 's stout and good
   May prove a jeopardie.

" What wouldst thou do, my squire so gay,
   That rides beside my reyne, —
Were ye Glenallan's Earl the day,
   And I were Roland Cheyne?

" To turn the rein were sin and shame,
   To fight were wondrous peril, —
What would ye do now, Roland Cheyne,
   Were ye Glenallan's Earl? "

" Were I Glenallan's Earl this tide,
   And ye were Roland Cheyne,
The spur should be in my horse's side,
   And the bridle upon his mane.

" If they hae twenty thousand blades,
   And we twice ten times ten,
Yet they hae but their tartan plaids,
   And we are mail-clad men.

" My horse shall ride through ranks sae rude,
   As through the moorland fern, —
Then ne'er let the gentle Norman blude
   Grow cauld for Highland kerne."

SIR WALTER SCOTT.

LOCHINVAR.

O, YOUNG Lochinvar is come out of the west,
Through all the wide Border his steed was the best ;
And save his good broadsword, he weapon had
none,
He rode all unarmed, and he rode all alone.
So faithful in love, and so dauntless in war,
There never was knight like the young Lochinvar.

He staid not for brake, and he stopped not for
stone,
He swam the Eske river where ford there was
none ;
But ere he alighted at Netherby gate,
The bride had consented, the gallant came late :
For a laggard in love, and a dastard in war,
Was to wed the fair Ellen of young Lochinvar.

So boldly he entered the Netherby Hall,
Among bridesmen and kinsmen, and brothers, and
all :
Then spake the bride's father, his hand on his
sword,

(For the poor craven bridegroom said never a
    word,)
" O come ye in peace here, or come ye in war,
Or to dance at our bridal, young Lord Lochinvar? "

" I long wooed your daughter, my suit you denied ;
Love swells like the Solway, but ebbs like its tide —
And now am I come, with this lost love of mine,
To lead but one measure, drink one cup of wine.
There are maidens in Scotland more lovely by far,
That would gladly be bride to the young Lochinvar."

The bride kissed the goblet : the knight took it up,
He quaffed off the wine, and he threw down the cup.
She looked down to blush, and she looked up to sigh,
With a smile on her lips and a tear in her eye.
He took her soft hand, ere her mother could bar, —
" Now tread we a measure ! " said young Lochinvar.

So stately his form, and so lovely her face,
That never a hall such a galliard did grace ;
While her mother did fret, and her father did
    fume,
And the bridegroom stood dangling his bonnet and
    plume ;

And the bride-maidens whispered, " 'T were better
    by far,
To have matched our fair cousin with young Loch-
    invar."

One touch to her hand, and one word in her ear,
When they reached the hall-door, and the charger
    stood near;
So light to the croupe the fair lady he swung,
So light to the saddle before her he sprung.
"She is won! we are gone over bank, bush and
    scaur;
"They 'll have fleet steeds that follow," quoth young
    Lochinvar.

There was mounting 'mong Graemes of the Nether-
    by clan;
Forsters, Fenwicks, and Musgraves, they rode and
    they ran:
There was racing and chasing on Cannobie Lee,
But the lost bride of Netherby ne'er did they see.
So daring in love, and so dauntless in war,
Have ye e'er heard of gallant like young Lochinvar?

Sir Walter Scott.

PIBROCH OF DONUIL DHU.

PIBROCH of Donuil Dhu,
   Pibroch of Donuil,
Wake thy wild voice anew,
   Summon Clan-Conuil.
Come away, come away,
   Hark to the summons !
Come in your war array,
   Gentles and commons.

Come from deep glen, and
   From mountain so rocky,
The war-pipe and pennon
   Are at Inverlocky.
Come every hill-plaid, and
   True heart that wears one,
Come every steel blade, and
   Strong hand that bears one.

Leave untended the herd,
   The flock without shelter ;
Leave the corpse uninterred,
   The bride at the altar ;

Leave the deer, leave the steer,
 Leave nets and barges :
Come with your fighting gear,
 Broadswords and targes.

Come as the winds come, when
 Forests are rended ;
Come as the waves come, when
 Navies are stranded :
Faster come, faster come,
 Faster and faster,
Chief, vassal, page, and groom,
 Tenant and master.

Fast they come, fast they come ;
 See how they gather !
Wide waves the eagle plume,
 Blended with heather.
Cast your plaids, draw your blades,
 Forward each man set !
Pibroch of Donuil Dhu,
 Knell for the onset !

SIR WALTER SCOTT.

FLODDEN-FIELD.

1513.

From " Marmion."

By this, though deep the evening fell,
Still rose the battle's deadly swell,
For still the Scots around their king,
Unbroken, fought in desperate ring.
Where 's now their victor vaward wing,
　Where Huntly, and where Home? —
Oh for a blast of that dread horn,
On Fontarabian echoes borne,
　That to King Charles did come,
When Rowland brave, and Olivier,
And every paladin and peer,
　On Roncesvalles died !
Such blast might warn them, not in vain
To quit the plunder of the slain,
And turn the doubtful day again,
　While yet on Flodden side,
Afar, the royal standard flies,
And round it toils, and bleeds, and dies,
　Our Caledonian pride !

In vain the wish — for far away,
While spoil and havoc mark their way,
Near Sybil's cross the plunderers stray.

.   .   .   .   .

More desperate grew the strife of death.
The English shafts in volleys hailed,
In headlong charge their horse assailed ;
Front, flank, and rear the squadrons sweep
To break the Scottish circle deep,
    That fought around their king.
But yet, though thick the shafts as snow,
Though charging knights like whirlwinds go,
Though bill-men ply the ghastly blow,
    Unbroken was the ring ;
The stubborn spear-men still made good
Their dark impenetrable wood,
Each stepping where his comrade stood,
    The instant that he fell.
No thought was there of dastard flight ;
Linked in the serried phalanx tight,
Groom fought like noble, squire like knight,
    As fearlessly and well ;
Till utter darkness closed her wing
O'er their thin host and wounded king.
Then skilful Surrey's sage commands
Led back from strife his shattered bands ;
    And from the charge they drew,

As mountain waves, from wasted lands,
   Sweep back to ocean blue.
Then did their loss his foemen know ;
Their king, their lords, their mightiest low,
They melted from the field as snow,
When streams are swoln and south winds blow,
   Dissolves in silent dew.
Tweed's echoes heard the ceaseless plash,
   While many a broken band,
Disordered through her currents dash,
   To gain the Scottish land ;
To town and tower, to down and dale,
To tell red Flodden's dismal tale,
And raise the universal wail.
Tradition, legend, tune, and song,
Shall many an age that wail prolong :
Still from the sire the son shall hear
Of the stern strife, and carnage drear,
   Of Flodden's fatal field,
Where shivered was fair Scotland's spear,
   And broken was her shield.

Day dawns upon the mountain's side : —
There, Scotland ! lay thy bravest pride,
Chiefs, knights, and nobles, many a one :
The sad survivors all are gone. —
View not that corpse mistrustfully,
Defaced and mangled though it be ;

Nor to yon Border castle high,
Look northward with upbraiding eye ;
   Nor cherish hope in vain,
That, journeying far on foreign strand,
The royal pilgrim to his land
   May yet return again.
He saw the wreck his rashness wrought ;
Reckless of life, he desperate fought,
   And fell on Flodden plain :
And well in death his trusty brand,
Firm clenched within his manly hand,
   Beseemed the monarch slain.

SIR WALTER SCOTT.

EDINBURGH AFTER FLODDEN.

SEPTEMBER, 1513.

NEWS of battle !—news of battle !
   Hark ! 't is ringing down the street ;
And the archways and the pavement
   Bear the clang of hurrying feet.
News of battle ! who hath brought it?
   News of triumph ! who should bring
Tidings from our noble army,
   Greetings from our gallant King?
All last night we watched the beacons
   Blazing on the hills afar,
Each one bearing, as it kindled,
   Message of the opened war.
All night long the northern steamers
   Shot across the trembling sky :
Fearful lights that never beckon,
   Save when kings or heroes die.

News of battle ! who hath brought it?
   All are thronging to the gate ;
" Warder — warder ! open quickly !
   Man — is this a time to wait?

And the heavy gates are opened ;
　　Then a murmur long and loud,
And a cry of fear and wonder
　　Bursts from out the bending crowd.
For they see in battered harness
　　Only one hard-stricken man ;
And his weary steed is wounded,
　　And his cheek is pale and wan :
Spearless hangs a bloody banner
　　In his weak and drooping hand —
God ! can that be Randolph Murray,
　　Captain of the city band?

Round him crush the people, crying,
　　" Tell us all — oh, tell us true !
Where are they who went to battle,
　　Randolph Murray, sworn to you?
Where are they, our brothers — children?
　　Have they met the English foe?
Why art thou alone, unfollowed?
　　Is it weal or is it woe?"
Like a corpse the grisly warrior
　　Looks from out his helm of steel;
But no word he speaks in answer —
　　Only with his arméd heel
Chides his weary steed, and onward
　　Up the city streets they ride, —

Fathers, sisters, mothers, children,
  Shrieking, praying, by his side.
" By the God that made thee, Randolph !
  Tell us what mischance hath come."
Then he lifts his riven banner,
  And the asker's voice is dumb.

The elders of the city
  Have met within their hall —
The men whom good King James had charged
  To watch the tower and wall.
" Your hands are weak with age," he said,
  " Your hearts are stout and true ;
So bide ye in the Maiden Town,
  While others fight for you.
My trumpet from the Border-side
  Shall send a blast so clear,
That all who wait within the gate
  That stirring sound may hear.
Or, if it be the will of heaven
  That back I never come,
And, if instead of Scottish shouts,
  Ye hear the English drum,—
Then let the warning bells ring out,
  Then gird you to the fray,
Then man the walls like burghers stout,
  And fight while fight you may.

'T were better that in fiery flame
　　The roofs should thunder down,
Than that the foot of foreign foe
　　Should trample in the town !"

Then in came Randolph Murray, —
　　His step was slow and weak,
And, as he doffed his dinted helm,
　　The tears ran down his cheek :
They fell upon his corslet
　　And on his mailèd hand,
As he gazed around him wistfully,
　　Leaning sorely on his brand ;
And none who then beheld him
　　But straight were smote with fear,
For a bolder and a sterner man
　　Had never couched a spear.
They knew so sad a messenger
　　Some ghastly news must bring ;
And all of them were fathers,
　　And their sons were with the King.

And up then rose the Provost —
　　A brave old man was he,
Of ancient name, and knightly fame,
　　And chivalrous degree.
He ruled our city like a Lord
　　Who brooked no equal here,

And ever for the townsman's rights
  Stood up 'gainst prince and peer.
And he had seen the Scottish host
  March from the Borough-muir,
With music-storm and clamorous shout,
  And all the din that thunders out
When youth 's of victory sure ;
  But yet a dearer thought had he, —
For, with a father's pride,
  He saw his last remaining son
Go forth by Randolph's side,
  With casque on head and spur on heel,
All keen to do and dare ;
  And proudly did that gallant boy
Dunedin's banner bear.
  Oh ! woful now was the old man's look,
And he spake right heavily ;
  "Now, Randolph, tell thy tidings,
However sharp they be !
  Woe is written on thy visage,
Death is looking from thy face ;
  Speak ! though it be of overthrow,
It cannot be disgrace !

Right bitter was the agony
  That wrung that soldier proud ;
Thrice did he strive to answer,
  And thrice he groaned aloud ;

Then he gave the riven banner
　　To the old man's shaking hand,
Saying : "That is all I bring ye
　　From the bravest of the land !
Ay ! ye may look upon it —
　　It was guarded well and long,
By your brothers and your children,
　　By the valiant and the strong.
One by one they fell around it,
　　As the archers laid them low,
Grimly dying, still unconquered,
　　With their faces to the foe.
Ay ! ye may well look upon it —
　　There is more than honor there ;
Else, be sure, I had not brought it
　　From the field of dark despair.
Never yet was royal banner
　　Steeped in such a costly dye ;
It hath lain upon a bosom
　　Where no other shroud shall lie.
Sirs, I charge you keep it holy,
　　Keep it as a sacred thing !
For the stain ye see upon it
　　Was the life-blood of your King !"

Woe, woe, and lamentation,
　　What a piteous cry was there !
Widows, maidens, mothers, children,
　　Shrieking, sobbing in despair !

Through the streets the death-word rushes,
  Spreading terror, sweeping on.
" Jesu Christ ! our King has fallen —
  O Great God, King James is gone !
Holy Mother Mary, shield us,
  Thou who erst didst lose thy Son !
O the blackest day for Scotland
  That she ever knew before !
O our King — the good, the noble,
  Shall we see him never more ?
Woe to us, and woe to Scotland !
  O our sons, our sons and men !
Surely some have 'scaped the Southron,
  Surely some will come again ! "
Till the oak that fell last winter
  Shall uprear its shattered stem,
Wives and mothers of Dunedin —
  Ye may look in vain for them !

But within the Council Chamber
  All was silent as the grave,
Whilst the tempest of their sorrow
  Shook the bosoms of the brave.
Well indeed might they be shaken
  With the weight of such a blow ;
He was gone — their prince, their idol,
  Whom they loved and worshipped so !

Like a knell of death and judgment,
　　Rung from heaven by angel hand,
Fell the words of desolation
　　On the elders of the land.
Hoary heads were bowed and trembling ;
　　Withered hands were clasped and wrung ;
God had left the old and feeble,
　　He had ta'en away the young.

Then the Provost he uprose,
　　And his lip was ashen white ;
But a flush was on his brow,
　　And his eye was full of light.
"Thou hast spoken, Randolph Murray,
　　Like a soldier stout and true ;
Thou hast done a deed of daring
　　Had been perilled but by few.
For thou hast not shamed to face us,
　　Nor to speak thy ghastly tale,
Standing — thou a knight and captain —
　　Here, alive within thy mail !
Now, as my God shall judge me,
　　I hold it braver done,
Than hadst thou tarried in thy place,
　　And died above my son !
Thou need'st not tell it : he is dead.
　　God help us all this day !

But speak — how fought the citizens
  Within the furious fray?
For, by the might of Mary,
  'T were something still to tell,
That no Scottish foot went backward
  When the Royal Lion fell!"

" No one failed him! He is keeping
  Royal state and semblance still;
Knight and noble lie around him,
  Cold on Flodden's fatal hill.
Of the brave and gallant-hearted,
  Whom ye sent with prayers away,
Not a single man departed
  From his Monarch yesterday.
Had you seen them, O my masters!
  When the night began to fall,
And the English spearmen gathered
  Round a grim and ghastly wall!
As the wolves in winter circle
  Round the leaguer on the heath,
So the greedy foe glared upward,
  Panting still for blood and death.
But a rampart rose before them,
  Which the boldest dare not scale:
Every stone a Scottish body,
  Every step a corpse in mail!

And behind it lay our Monarch,
  Clenching still his shivered sword ;
By his side Montrose and Athole,
  At his feet a Southron lord.
All so thick they lay together,
  When the stars lit up the sky,
That I knew not who were stricken,
  Or who yet remained to die.

Few there were when Surrey halted,
  And his wearied host withdrew ;
None but dying men around me,
  When the English trumpet blew.
Then I stooped and took the banner,
  As you see it from his breast,
And I closed our hero's eyelids
  And I left him to his rest.
In the mountain growled the thunder,
  As I leaped the woful wall,
And the heavy clouds were settling
  Over Flodden like a pall.

        .   .   .   .   .

                              WM. E. AYTOUN.

BORDER BALLAD.

SIXTEENTH CENTURY.

MARCH, march, Ettrick and Teviotdale,
   Why the deil dinna ye march forward in order?
March, march, Eskdale and Liddesdale,
   All the Blue Bonnets are bound for the Border.
        Many a banner spread
        Flutters above your head,
Many a crest that is famous in story ;
        Mount and make ready then,
        Sons of the mountain glen,
Fight for the Queen and our old Scottish glory.

Come from the hills where the hirsels are grazing,
   Come from the glen of the buck and the roe ;
Come to the crag where the beacon is blazing,
   Come with the buckler, the lance, and the bow.
        Trumpets are sounding,
        War-steeds are bounding,
Stand to your arms then, and march in good order ;
        England shall many a day
        Tell of the bloody fray,
When the Blue Bonnets came over the Border !

SIR WALTER SCOTT.

JAMIE TELFER

OF THE FAIR DODHEAD.

IT fell about the Martinmas [1] tide,
 When our Border steeds get corn and hay,
The Captain of Bencastle hath bound him to ride,
 And he 's ower to Tividale to drive a prey.

The first ae guide that they met wi',
 It was high up in Hardhaughswire ;
The second guide that they met wi',
 It was laigh down in Borthwick water.

" What tidings, what tidings, my trusty guide ? "
 " Nae tidings, nae tidings, I hae to thee ;
But gin ye 'll gae to the fair Dodhead,
 Mony a cow's cauf I 'll let thee see."

And when they came to the fair Dodhead,
 Right hastily they clam the peel ; [2]
They loosed the kye out ane and a',
 And ramshackled [3] the house right weel.

---

[1] *Martinmas,* — November 11.
[2] *Peel,* — stronghold where the cattle were kept.
[3] *Ramshackled,* — ransacked.

Now Jamie Telfer's heart was sair,
   The tear aye rowing in his e'e ;
He pled wi' the Captain to hae his gear,
   Or else revenged he wad be.

The Captain turned him round and leugh ;[1]
   Said, — " Man, there 's naething in thy house,
But ae auld sword without a sheath,
   That hardly now would fell a mouse."

The sun wasna up, but the moon was down,
   It was the gryming[2] of a new-fa'n snaw,
Jamie Telfer has run ten miles a-foot,
   Between the Dodhead and the Stobs's Ha'.

And when he cam to the fair tower gate,
   He shouted loud, and cried weel high,
Till out bespak auld Gibby Elliot —
   " Whae 's this that brings the fray to me?"

" It 's I, Jamie Telfer, o' the fair Dodhead,
   And a harried[3] man I think I be !
There 's naething left at the fair Dodhead,
   But a waefu' wife and bairnies three."

[1] *Leugh,* — laughed.
[2] *Gryming,* — sprinkling.
[3] *Harried,* — plundered.

" Gae seek your succor at Branksome Ha',
    For succour ye 'se get nane frae me !
Gae seek your succour where ye paid black-mail,
    For man, ye ne'er paid money to me."

Jamie has turned him round about,
    I wat the tear blinded his e'e —
" I 'll ne'er pay mail to Elliot again,
    And the fair Dodhead I 'll never see !

" My hounds may a' rin masterless,
    My hawks may fly frae tree to tree,
My lord may grip my vassal lands,
    For there again maun I never be."

He has turned him to the Tiviot side,
    E'en as fast as he could drie,
Till he cam to the Coultart Cleugh,
    And there he shouted baith loud and high.

Then up bespak him auld Jock Grieve, —
    " Whae 's this that brings the fray to me?"
" It 's I, Jamie Telfer, o' the fair Dodhead,
    A harried man I trow I be."

" There 's naething left in the fair Dodhead,
    But a greeting wife and bairnies three,
And sax poor calves stand in the stall,
    A' routing loud for their minnie." [1]

[1] *Minnie*, — mother.

" Alack a wae ! " quo' auld Jock Grieve, —
 " Alack ! my heart is sair for thee !
For I was married on the elder sister,
 And you on the youngest o' a' the three."

Then he has ta'en out a bonny black,
 Was right weel fed wi' corn and hay,
And he 's set Jamie Telfer on his back,
 To the Catslockhill to tak the fray.

And whan he cam to the Catslockhill,
 He shouted loud, and cried weel high,
Till out and spak him William's Wat,
 " O whae 's this brings the fray to me ? "

" It 's I, Jamie Telfer, o' the fair Dodhead,
 A harried man I think I be !
The Captain o' Bewcastle has driven my gear ;
 For God's sake, rise and succor me ! "

" Alas for wae ! " quoth William's Wat,
 " Alack, for thee my heart is sair !
I never cam by the fair Dodhead,
 That ever I fand thy basket bare."

He 's set his twa sons on coal-black steeds,
 Himsell upon a freckled gray,
And they are on wi' Jamie Telfer,
 To Branksome Ha' to tak the fray.

And when they cam to Branksome Ha'
　　They shouted a' baith loud and high,
Till up and spak him auld Buccleuch,
　　Said, "Whae 's this brings the fray to me?"

"It 's I, Jamie Telfer, o' the fair Dodhead,
　　And a harried man I think I be !
There 's nought left in the fair Dodhead,
　　But a greeting wife and bairnies three."

"Alack for wae !" quoth the gude auld lord,
　　And ever my heart is wae for thee !
But fye gar cry on Willie, my son,
　　And see that he come to me speedilie !

"Gar warn the water [1] braid and wide,
　　Gar warn it soon and hastilie !
They that winna ride for Telfer's kye,
　　Let them never look in the face o' me !

"Warn Wat o' Harden, and his sons,
　　Wi' them will Borthwick Water ride ;
Warn Gaudilands, and Allanhaugh,
　　And Gilmanscleugh and Commonside.

[1] The water, in the mountainous districts of Scotland,
is often used to express the banks of the river, which are
the only inhabitable parts of the country. To raise the
water, therefore, was to alarm those who lived along its
side.

" Ride by the gate at Priesthaughswire,
　　And warn the Currors of the Lee ;
As ye come down the Hermitage Slack,
　　Warn doughty Willie o' Gorrinberry."

The Scotts they rade, the Scotts they ran,
　　Sae starkly and sae steadilie !
And aye the ower-word o' the thrang
　　Was —" Rise for Branksome readilie ! "

The gear was driven the Frostylee up,
　　Frae the Frostylee unto the plain,
Whan Willie has looked his men before,
　　And saw the kye right fast drivand.

" Whae drives thir kye? " 'gan Willie say,
　　" To make an outspeckle [1] o' me ? "
" It 's I, the Captain o' Bewcastle, Willie ;
　　I winna layne [2] my name for thee."

" O will ye let Telfer's kye gae back,
　　Or will ye do aught for regard o' me ?
Or, by the faith o' my body," quo' Willie Scott,
　　" I 'se ware my dame's cauf skin on thee ! "

" I winna let the kye gae back,
　　Neither for thy love, nor yet thy fear ;
But I will drive Jamie Telfer's kye,
　　In spite of every Scott that 's here."

---

[1] *Outspeckle,* — laughing-stock.　　[2] *Layne,* — conceal.

" Set on them, lads ! " quo' Willie then ;
　　Fye lads, set on them cruellie !
For, ere they win to the Ritterford,
　　Mony a toom [1] saddle there sall be ! "

Then til't they gaed wi' heart and hand,
　　The blows fell thick as bickering hail ;
And mony a horse ran masterless,
　　And mony a comely cheek was pale.

But Willie was stricken o'er the head,
　　And through the knapscap [2] the sword has
　　　gane ;
And Harden grat [3] for very rage,
　　When Willie on the ground lay slain.

But he 's ta'en aff his gude steel cap,
　　And thrice he 's waved it in the air —
The Dinlay snaw was ne'er mair white
　　Nor the lyart [4] locks of Harden's hair.

" Revenge ! revenge ! " auld Wat 'gan cry ;
　　" Fye, lads, lay on them cruellie !
We 'll ne'er see Tiviotside again,
　　Or Willie's death revenged sall be."

[1] *Toom,* — empty.　　　[2] *Knapscap,* — headpiece.
[3] *Grat,* — wept.　　　　[4] *Lyart,* — hoary.

O mony a horse ran masterless,
  The splintered lances flew on high ;
But or they wan to the Kershope ford,
  The Scotts had gotten the victory.

John o' Brigham there was slain,
  And John o' Barlow, as I heard say ;
And thirty mae o' the Captain's men
  Lay bleeding on the ground that day.

Then word is gane to the Captain's bride,
  Even in the lower where that she lay,
That her lord was prisoner in enemy's land,
  Since into Tividale he had led the way.

" I wad lourd [1] have had a winding-sheet,
  And helped to put it o'er his head,
Ere he had been disgraced by the Border
        Scot,
  When he ower Liddel his men did lead."

There was a wild gallant amang us a',
  His name was Watty with the Wudspurs [2],
Cried — " On for his house in Stanegirthside,
  If ony man will ride with us ! "

---

[1] *Lourd*, — liefer, rather.
[2] *Wudspurs*, — hotspur, or madspur.

When they cam to the Stanegirthside,
    They dang wi' trees, and burst the door ;
They loosed out a' the captain's kye,
    And set them forth our lads before.

There was an auld wife ayont the fire,
    A wee bit o' the Captain's kin —
"Whae daur loose out the Captain's kye ?
    Or answer to him and his men ? "

" It 's I, Watty Wudspurs, loose the kye,
    I winna layne my name frae thee !
And I will loose out the Captain's kye,
    In scorn of a' his men and he."

When they cam to the fair Dodhead,
    They were a welcome sight to see !
For instead of his ain ten milk kye,
    Jamie Telfer has gotten thirty and three.

And he has paid the rescue shot,
    Baith wi' goud and white monie ;
And at the burial of Willie Scott,
    I wot was mony a weeping e'e.

                    SCOTT'S MINSTRELSY OF THE SCOTTISH BORDER.

IVRY.

1590

Now glory to the Lord of Hosts, from whom all
glories are !
And glory to our Sovereign Liege, King Henry of
Navarre !
Now let there be the merry sound of music and of
dance,
Through thy corn-fields green, and sunny vines, O
pleasant land of France.
And thou Rochelle, our own Rochelle, proud city
of the waters,
Again let rapture light the eyes of all thy mourning
daughters.
As thou wert constant in our ills, be joyous in our
joy,
For cold, and stiff, and still are they who wrought
thy walls annoy.
Hurrah ! Hurrah ! a single field hath turned the
chance of war,
Hurrah ! Hurrah ! for Ivry, and Henry of Navarre.

Oh ! how our hearts were beating, when, at the
    dawn of day,
We saw the army of the League drawn out in long
    array ;
With all its priest-led citizens, and all its rebel
    peers,
And Appenzel's stout infantry, and Egmont's Flem-
    ish spears.
There rode the brood of false Lorraine, the curses
    of our land ;
And dark Mayenne was in their midst, a truncheon
    in his hand :
And, as we looked on them, we thought of Seine's
    empurpled flood,
And good Coligni's hoary hair all dabbled with his
    blood ;
And we cried unto the living God, who rules the
    fate of war,
To fight for his own holy name, and Henry of
    Navarre.

The King is come to marshal us, in all his armor
    drest,
And he has bound a snow-white plume upon his
    gallant crest.
He looked upon his people and a tear was in his
    eye ;

He looked upon the traitors, and his glance was
stern and high.

Right graciously he smiled on us, as rolled from
wing to wing,

Down all our line, a deafening shout, " God save
our Lord the King."

" And if my standard-bearer fall, as fall full well he
may,

For never saw I promise yet of such a bloody fray,

Press where ye see my white plume shine, amidst
the ranks of war,

And be your oriflamme to-day the helmet of
Navarre."

Hurrah ! the foes are moving. Hark to the mingled din,

Of fife, and steed, and trump, and drum, and roaring culverin.

The fiery Duke is pricking fast across Saint André's
plain,

With all the hireling chivalry of Guelders and
Almayne.

Now by the lips of those ye love, fair gentlemen
of France,

Charge for the golden lilies, — upon them with the
lance.

A thousand spurs are striking deep, a thousand
spears in rest,

A thousand knights are pressing close behind the
    snow-white crest;
And in they burst, and on they rushed, while, like
    a guiding star,
Amidst the thickest carnage blazed the helmet of
    Navarre.

Now, God be praised, the day is ours.   Mayenne
    hath turned his rein.
D'Aumale hath cried for quarter.   The Flemish
    count is slain.
Their ranks are breaking like thin clouds before a
    Biscay gale;
The field is heaped with bleeding steeds, and flags,
    and cloven mail,
And then we thought on vengeance, and all along
    our van,
"Remember Saint Bartholomew," was passed from
    man to man.
But out spake gentle Henry, "No Frenchman is
    my foe:
Down, down with every foreigner, but let your
    brethren go."
Oh! was there ever such a knight, in friendship
    or in war,
As our Sovereign Lord, King Henry, the soldier of
    Navarre?

Right well fought all the Frenchmen who fought
  for France to-day;
And many a lordly banner God gave them for a
  prey;
But we of the religion have borne us best in fight;
And the good Lord of Rosny hath ta'en the cornet
  white.
Our own true Maximilian, the cornet white hath
  ta'en,
The cornet white with crosses black, the flag of
  false Lorraine.
Up with it high; unfurl it wide; that all the host
  may know
How God hath humbled the proud house which
  wrought his church such woe;
Then on the ground, while trumpets sound their
  loudest point of war,
Fling the red shreds, a foot-cloth meet for Henry
  of Navarre.

Ho! maidens of Vienna; Ho! matrons of Lu-
  cerne;
Weep, weep, and rend your hair for those who
  never shall return.
Ho! Philip, send, for charity, thy Mexican pistoles,
That Antwerp monks may sing a mass for thy poor
  spearmen's souls.

Ho ! gallant nobles of the League, look that your
arms be bright ;

Ho ! burghers of Saint Genevieve, keep watch and
ward to-night.

For our God hath crushed the tyrant, our God hath
raised the slave,

And mocked the counsel of the wise, and the valor
of the brave.

Then glory to his holy name, from whom all glories
are,

And glory to our Sovereign Lord, King Henry of
Navarre.

THOMAS BABINGTON MACAULAY.

THE REVENGE.

AUGUST, 1591.

AT Flores in the Azores, Sir Richard Grenville lay,
And a pinnace, like a fluttered bird, came flying
    from far away :
" Spanish ships-of-war at sea ! we have sighted
    fifty-three ! "
Then sware Lord Thomas Howard : " 'Fore God I
    am no coward ;
But I cannot meet them here, for my ships are out
    of gear,
And the half my men are sick. I must fly, but
    follow quick.
We are six ships of the line ; can we fight with
    fifty-three ? "

Then spake Sir Richard Grenville : " I know you are
    no coward ;
You fly them for a moment to fight with them again.
But I 've ninety men and more that are lying sick
    ashore.

I should count myself the coward if I left them, my
    Lord Howard,
To these Inquisition dogs and the devildoms of
    Spain."

So Lord Howard past away with five ships of war
    that day,
Till he melted like a cloud in the silent summer
    heaven ;
But Sir Richard bore in hand all his sick men from
    the land
Very carefully and slow,
Men of Bideford in Devon,
And we laid them on the ballast down below ;
For we brought them all aboard,
And they blest him in their pain, that they were
    not left to Spain,
To the thumbscrew and the stake, for the glory of
    the Lord.

He had only a hundred seamen to work the ship
    and to fight,
And he sailed away from Flores till the Spaniard
    came in sight,
With his huge sea-castles heaving upon the weather
    bow.

" Shall we fight or shall we fly?
Good Sir Richard, tell us now,
For to fight is but to die !
There 'll be little of us left by the time this sun be set."
And Sir Richard said again : " We be all good
    English men.
Let us bang these dogs of Seville, the children of
    the devil,
For I never turned my back upon Don or devil yet."

Sir Richard spoke and he laughed, and we roared a
    hurrah, and so
The little Revenge ran on sheer into the heart of
    the foe,
With her hundred fighters on deck, and her ninety
    sick below ;
For half of their fleet to the right and half to the
    left were seen,
And the little Revenge ran on through the long sea-
    lane between.

Thousands of their soldiers looked down from their
    decks and laughed,
Thousands of their seamen made mock at the mad
    little craft
Running on and on, till delayed

By their mountain-like San Philip that, of fifteen
    hundred tons,
And up-shadowing high above us with her yawning
    tiers of guns,
Took the breath from our sails, and we stayed.

And while now the great San Philip hung above us
    like a cloud,
Whence the thunderbolt will fall
Long and loud,
Four galleons drew away
From the Spanish fleet that day,
And two upon the larboard and two upon the star-
    board lay,
And the battie-thunder broke from them all.

But anon the great San Philip, she bethought her-
    self and went,
Having that within her womb that had left her ill-
    content ;
And the rest they came aboard us, and they fought
    us hand to hand,
For a dozen times they came with their pikes and
    musqueteers,
And a dozen times we shook 'em off as a dog that
    shakes his ears,
When he leaps from the water to the land.

And the sun went down, and the stars came out far
    over the summer sea,
But never a moment ceased the fight of the one
    and the fifty-three.
Ship after ship, the whole night long, their high-
    built galleons came,
Ship after ship, the whole night long, with her
    battle-thunder and flame ;
Ship after ship, the whole night long, drew back
    with her dead and her shame.
For some were sunk and many were shattered, and
    so could fight us no more —
God of battles, was ever a battle like this in the
    world before ?

For he said " Fight on ! fight on ! "
Though his vessel was all but a wreck ;
And it chanced that, when half of the summer night
    was gone,
With a grisly wound to be drest, he had left the
    deck,
But a bullet struck him that was dressing it sud-
    denly dead,
And himself, he was wounded again in the side and
    the head.
And he said " Fight on ! fight on ! "

And the night went down, and the sun smiled out
    far over the summer sea,
And the Spanish fleet with broken sides lay round
    us all in a ring;
But they dared not touch us again, for they feared
    that we still could sting,
So they watched what the end would be.
And we had not fought them in vain,
But in perilous plight were we,
Seeing forty of our poor hundred were slain,
And half of the rest of us maimed for life
In the crash of the cannonades and the desperate
    strife;
And the sick men down in the hold were most of
    them stark and cold,
And the pikes were all broken or bent, and the
    powder was all of it spent;
And the masts and the rigging were lying over the side;
But Sir Richard cried in his English pride,
" We have fought such a fight, for a day and a night,
As may never be fought again!
We have won great glory, my men!
And a day less or more
At sea or ashore,
We die — does it matter when?
Sink me the ship, Master Gunner — sink her, split
    her in twain!
Fall into the hands of God, not into the hands of
    Spain! "

And the gunner said " Ay, ay," but the seamen
    made reply :
" We have children, we have wives,
And the Lord hath spared our lives.
We will make the Spaniard promise, if we yield, to
    let us go ;
We shall live to fight again and to strike another blow."
And the lion there lay dying, and they yielded to
    the foe.

And the stately Spanish men to their flagship bore
    him then,
Where they laid him by the mast, old Sir Richard
    caught at last,
And they praised him to his face with their courtly
    foreign grace ;
But he rose upon their decks, and he cried :
" I have fought for Queen and Faith like a valiant
    man and true ;
I have only done my duty as a man is bound to do :
With a joyful spirit I, Sir Richard Grenville, die ! "
And he fell upon their decks, and he died.

And they stared at the dead that had been so
    valiant and true,
And had holden the power and glory of Spain so
    cheap

That he dared her with one little ship and his
    English few ;

Was he devil or man? He was devil for aught
    they knew,

But they sank his body with honor down into the
    deep,

And they manned the Revenge with a swarthier,
    alien crew,

And away she sailed with her loss and longed for
    her own ;

When a wind from the lands they had ruined awoke
    from sleep,

And the water began to heave and the weather to
    moan,

And or ever that evening ended, a great gale blew,

And a wave like the wave that is raised by an earth-
    quake grew,

Till it smote on their hulls and their sails and their
    masts and their flags,

And the whole sea plunged and fell on the shot-
    shattered navy of Spain,

And the little Revenge herself went down by the
    island crags,

To be lost evermore in the main.

ALFRED TENNYSON.

KINMONT WILLIE.

1596.

O HAVE ye na heard o' the fause Sakelde?
   O have ye na heard o' the keen Lord Scroope?
How they hae ta'en bauld Kinmont Willie,
   On Haribee [1] to hang him up?

Had Willie had but twenty men,
   But twenty men as stout as he;
Fause Sakelde had never the Kinmont ta'en,
   Wi' eight score in his companie.

They band his legs beneath the steed,
   They tied his hands behind his back;
They guarded him, fivesome on each side,
   And they brought him ower the Liddel-rack. [2]

[1] Haribee is the place of execution at Carlisle.
[2] A ford on the Liddel.

They led him through the Liddel-rack,
    And also through the Carlisle sands ;
They brought him to Carlisle Castell,
    To be at my Lord Scroope's commands.

"My hands are tied, but my tongue is free,
    And whae will dare this deed avow?
Or answer by the Border law?
    Or answer to the bauld Buccleuch?"

"Now haud thy tongue, thou rank reiver ![1]
    There 's never a Scot shall set thee free :
Before ye cross my castle gate,
    I trow ye shall take farewell o' me !"

"Fear na ye that, my lord," quo' Willie :
    "By the faith o' my body, Lord Scroope,"
        he said, —
"I never yet lodged in a hostelrie,
    But I paid my lawing[2] before I gaed."

Now word is gane to the bauld Keeper,
    In Branksome Ha' where that he lay,
That Lord Scroope has ta'en the Kinmont Willie,
    Between the hours of night and day.

[1] *Reiver*, — robber.
[2] *Lawing*, — reckoning.

He has ta'en the table wi' his hand,
    He garred the red wine spring on hie, —
" Now, Christ's curse on my head," he said,
    " But avenged of Lord Scroope I'll be !

" O is my basnet [1] a widow's curch ? [2]
    Or my lance a wand of the willow-tree ?
Or my arm a ladye's lilye hand,
    That an English lord should lightly [3] me ?

" And have they ta'en him, Kinmont Willie,
    Against the truce of Border tide,
And forgotten that the bauld Buccleuch
    Is Keeper here on the Scottish side ?

" And have they e'en ta'en him, Kinmont Willie,
    Withouten either dread or fear ?
And forgotten that the bauld Buccleuch
    Can back a steed, or shake a spear ?

" O were there war between the lands,
    As weel I wot that there is none,
I would slight Carlisle Castell high,
    Though it were builded of marble stone.

[1] *Basnet*, — helmet.   [2] *Curch*, — coif.
        [3] *Lightly*, — set light by.

" I would set that castell in a low,[1]
    And sloken it with English blood !
There 's never a man in Cumberland
    Should ken where Carlisle Castell stood.

"But since nae war 's between the lands,
    And there is peace, and peace should be ;
I 'll neither harm English lad nor lass,
    And yet the Kinmont freed shall be !"

He has called him forty Marchmen bauld,
    I trow they were of his ain name,
Except Sir Gilbert Elliot, called
    The Laird of Stobs, I mean the same.

He has called him forty Marchmen bauld,
    Were kinsmen to the bauld Buccleuch,
With spur on heel, and splent on spauld,[2]
    And gleuves of green, and feathers blue.

There were five and five before them a',
    Wi' hunting-horns and bugles bright :
And five and five came wi' Buccleuch,
    Like warden's men, arrayed for fight.

[1] Flame.
[2] *Splent on spauld,* — armor on shoulder.

And five and five, like a mason-gang,
   That carried the ladders lang and hie ;
And five and five, like broken men,[1]
   And so they reached the Woodhouselee.

And as we crossed the Bateable Land,
   When to the English side we held,
The first o' men that we met wi',
   Whae sould it be but fause Sakelde?

" Where be ye gaun, ye hunters keen? "
   Quo' fause Sakelde ; "come, tell to me ! " —
" We go to hunt an English stag,
   Has trespassed on the Scots countrie."

" Where be ye gaun, ye marshal men? "
   Quo' fause Sakelde ; " come tell me true ! " —
" We go to catch a rank reiver,
   Has broken faith wi' the bauld Buccleuch."

" Where are ye gaun, ye mason lads,
   Wi' a' your ladders lang and hie? " —
" We gang to herry a corbie's nest,
   That wons not far from Woodhouselee." —

" Where be ye gaun, ye broken men? "
   Quo' fause Sakelde ; " come, tell to me ! " —
Now Dickie o' Dryhope led that band,
   And the nevir a word of lear[2] had he.

---

[1] *Broken men,* — outlawed men.   [2] *Lear,* — lore.

" Why trespass ye on the English side?
    Row-footed outlaws, stand ! " quo' he ;
The nevir a word had Dickie to say,
    Sae he thrust the lance through his fause bodie.

Then on we held for Carlisle town,
    And at Staneshaw-bank the Eden we crossed ;
The water was great and meikle of spait,[1]
    But the nevir a horse nor man we lost.

And when we reached the Staneshaw-bank,
    The wind was rising loud and hie ;
And there the Laird garred leave our steeds,
    For fear that they should stamp and nie.

And when we left the Staneshaw-bank,
    The wind began full loud to blaw ;
But 't was wind and weet, and fire and sleet,
    When we came beneath the castle wa'.

We crept on knees, and held our breath,
    Till we placed the ladders against the wa',
And sae ready was Buccleuch himsell
    To mount the first before us a'.

He has ta'en the watchman by the throat,
    He flung him down upon the lead —
" Had there not been peace between our lands,
    Upon the other side thou hadst gaed ! "

[1] *Spait,* — flood.

" Now, sound out trumpets !"—quo' Buccleuch ;
  " Let 's waken Lord Scroope right merrilie !"
Then loud. the warden's trumpet blew —
  " *O whae dare meddle wi' me?* " [1]

Then speedilie to wark we gaed,
  And raised the slogan ane and a',
And cut a hole through a sheet of lead,
  And so we wan to the castle ha'.

They thought King James and a' his men
  Had won the house wi' bow and spear;
It was but twenty Scots and ten,
  That put a thousand in sic a stear ! [2]

Wi' coulters, and wi' fore-hammers,
  We garred the bars bang merrilie,
Until we came to the inner prison,
  Where Willie o' Kinmont he did lie.

And when we came to the lower prison,
  Where Willie o' Kinmont he did lie —
" O sleep ye, wake ye, Kinmont Willie,
  Upon the morn that thou 's to die ? " —

    [1] The name of a Border tune.
    [2] *Stear,* — stir.

"O I sleep saft,[1] and I wake aft;
  It's lang since sleeping was fleyed[2] frae me.
Gie my service back to my wife and bairns,
  And a' gude fellows that speir[3] for me." —

Then Red Rowan has hente him up,
  The starkest man in Teviotdale —
"Abide, abide now Red Rowan,
  Till of my Lord Scroope I take farewell.

"Farewell, farewell, my gude Lord Scroope!
  My gude Lord Scroope, farewell!" he cried —
"I'll pay you for my lodging maill,[4]
  When first we meet on the Border side:"

Then shoulder high with shout and cry,
  We bore him down the ladder lang;
At every stride Red Rowan made,
  I wot the Kinmont's airns[5] played clang!

"O mony a time," quo' Kinmont Willie,
  "I have ridden horse baith wild and wood;
But a rougher beast than Red Rowan
  I ween my legs have ne'er bestrode.

[1] *Saft*, — light.   [2] *Fleyed*, — frightened.
[3] *Speir*, — inquire.   [4] *Maill*, — rent.
              [5] *Airns*, — irons.

"And mony a time," quo' Kinmont Willie,
  "I 've pricked a horse out ower the furrs;[1]
But since the day I backed a steed,
  I never wore sic cumbrous spurs!"

We scarce had won the Staneshaw-bank,
  When a' the Carlisle bells were rung,
And a thousand men on horse and foot,
  Cam wi' the keen Lorde Scroope along.

Buccleuch has turned to Eden Water,
  Even where it flowed frae bank to brim,
And he has plunged in wi' a' his band,
  And safely swam them through the stream.

He turned him on the other side,
  And at Lord Scroope his glove flung he —
"If ye like na my visit in merry England,
  In fair Scotland come visit me!"

All sore astonished stood Lord Scroope,
  He stood as still as rock of stane;
He scarcely dared to trew[2] his eyes,
  When through the water they had gane.

---

[1] *Furrs,* — furze, or furrows?
[2] *Trew,* — trust.

" He is either himsell a devil frae hell,
    Or else his mother a witch maun be ;
I wadna have ridden that wan [1] water
    For a' the gowd in Christentie."

Scott's Minstrelsy of the Scottish Border.

[1] *Wan,* — pale, black, dark.

"HOW THEY BROUGHT THE GOOD NEWS FROM GHENT TO AIX."

[16 —]

I SPRANG to the stirrup, and Joris, and he ;
I galloped, Dirck galloped, we galloped all three ;
" Good speed !" cried the watch, as the gate-bolts
    undrew ;
" Speed !" echoed the wall to us galloping through ;
Behind shut the postern, the lights sank to rest,
And into the midnight we galloped abreast.

Not a word to each other ; we kept the great pace,
Neck by neck, stride by stride, never changing our
    place ;
I turned in my saddle and made its girths tight,
Then shortened each stirrup, and set the pique
    right,
Rebuckled the cheek-strap, chained slacker the bit,
Nor galloped less steadily Roland a whit.

'T was moonset at starting; but while we drew near
Lokeren, the cocks crew and twilight dawned
    clear;
At Boom, a great yellow star came out to see;
At Düffeld, 't was morning as plain as could be;
And from Mecheln church-steeple we heard the
    half-chime,
So Joris broke silence with, " Yet there is time ! "

At Aerschot, up leaped of a sudden the sun,
And against him the cattle stood black every one,
To stare through the mist at us galloping past,
And I saw my stout galloper Roland at last,
With resolute shoulders, each butting away
The haze, as some bluff river headland its spray.

And his low head and crest, just one sharp ear bent
    back
For my voice, and the other pricked out on his
    track;
And one eye's black intelligence, — ever that
    glance
O'er its white edge at me, his own master, askance !
And the thick heavy spume-flakes which aye and
    anon
His fierce lips shook upwards in galloping on.

By Hasselt, Dirck groaned; and cried Joris, "Stay
    spur !
Your Roos galloped bravely, the fault 's not in her,
We 'll remember at Aix " — for one heard the
    quick wheeze
Of her chest, saw the stretched neck and staggering
    knees,
And sunk tail, and horrible heave of the flank,
As down on her haunches she shuddered and sank.

So we were left galloping, Joris and I,
Past Looz and past Tongres, no cloud in the sky;
The broad sun above laughed a pitiless laugh,
'Neath our feet broke the brittle bright stubble like
    chaff;
Till over by Dalhem a dome-spire sprang white,
And "Gallop," gasped Joris, "for Aix is in sight !"

"How they 'll greet us !" and all in a moment his
    roan
Rolled neck and croup over, lay dead as a stone ;
And there was my Roland to bear the whole weight
Of the news which alone could save Aix from her
    fate,
With his nostrils like pits full of blood to the brim,
And with circles of red for his eye-sockets' rim.

Then I cast loose my buff-coat, each holster let fall,
Shook off both my jack-boots, let go belt and all,
Stood up in the stirrup, leaned, patted his ear,
Called my Roland his pet-name, my horse without
   peer;
Clapped my hands, laughed and sang, any noise,
   bad or good,
Till at length into Aix, Roland galloped and stood.

And all I remember is friends flocking round,
As I sat with his head 'twixt my knees on the
   ground,
And no voice but was praising this Roland of mine,
As I poured down his throat our last measure of
   wine,
Which (the burgesses voted by common consent)
Was no more than his due who brought good news
   from Ghent.

Robert Browning.

THE CAVALIER'S ESCAPE.

TRAMPLE ! trample ! went the roan,
   Trap ! trap ! went the gray ;
But pad ! *pad !* PAD ! like a thing that was mad,
   My chestnut broke away.
It was just five miles from Salisbury town,
   And but one hour to day.

Thud ! THUD ! came on the heavy roan,
   Rap ! RAP ! the mettled gray ;
But my chestnut mare was of blood so rare,
   That she showed them all the way.
Spur on ! spur on ! — I doffed my hat,
   And wished them all good-day.

They splashed through miry rut and pool,—
   Splintered through fence and rail ;
But chestnut Kate switched over the gate,—
   I saw them droop and tail.
To Salisbury town — but a mile of down,
   Once over this brook and rail.

Trap ! trap ! I heard their echoing hoofs
  Past the walls of mossy stone ;
The roan flew on at a staggering pace,
  But blood is better than bone.
I patted old Kate, and gave her the spur,
  For I knew it was all my own.

But trample ! trample ! came their steeds,
  And I saw their wolf's eyes burn ;
I felt like a royal hart at bay,
  And made me ready to turn.
I looked where highest grew the May,
  And deepest arched the fern.

I flew at the first knave's sallow throat ;
  One blow, and he was down.
The second rogue fired twice, and missed ;
  I sliced the villain's crown,—
Clove through the rest, and flogged brave Kate,
  Fast, fast to Salisbury town !

Pad ! pad ! they came on the level sward,
  Thud ! thud ! upon the sand,—
With a gleam of swords and a burning match,
  And a shaking of flag and hand ;
But one long bound, and I passed the gate,
  Safe from the canting band.

                              WALTER THORNBURY.

THE CAVALIER'S SONG.

A STEED ! a steed of matchlesse speed,
   A sword of metal keene !
All else to noble heartes is drosse,
   All else on earth is meane.
The neighyinge of the war-horse prowde,
   The rowlinge of the drum,
The clangor of the trumpet lowde,
   Be soundes from heaven that come ;
And O ! the thundering presse of knightes,
   Whenas their war-cryes swell,
May tole from heaven an angel bright,
   And rouse a fiend from hell.

Then mounte ! then mounte, brave gallants all,
   And don your helmes amaine ;
Death's couriers, Fame and Honor, call
   Us to the field againe.
No shrewish teares shall fill our eye
   When the sword-hilt 's in our hand —

Heart-whole we'll part, and no whit sighe
　　For the fayrest of the land ;
Let piping swaine, and craven wight,
　　Thus weepe and puling crye ;
Our business is like men to fight,
　　And hero-like to die.

WILLIAM MOTHERWELL.

THE EXECUTION OF MONTROSE.

1650.

Come hither, Evan Cameron !
   Come, stand beside my knee —
I hear the river roaring down
   Towards the wintry sea.
There 's shouting on the mountain-side,
   There 's war within the blast —
Old faces look upon me,
   Old forms go trooping past.
I hear the pibroch wailing
   Amidst the din of fight,
And my dim spirit wakes again
   Upon the verge of night.

'T was I that led the Highland host
   Through wild Lochaber's snows,
What time the plaided clans came down
   To battle with Montrose.
I 've told thee how the Southrons fell
   Beneath the broad claymore,

And how we smote the Campbell clan
　　By Inverlochy's shore.
I 've told thee how we swept Dundee,
　　And tamed the Lindsays' pride,
But never have I told thee yet
　　How the great Marquis died.

A traitor sold him to his foes, —
　　O deed of deathless shame !
I charge thee, boy, if e'er thou meet
　　With one of Assynt's name —
Be it upon the mountain's side,
　　Or yet within the glen,
Stand he in martial gear alone,
　　Or backed by armèd men —
Face him, as thou wouldst face the man
　　Who wronged thy sire's renown ;
Remember of what blood thou art,
　　And strike the caitiff down !

They brought him to the Watergate,
　　Hard bound with hempen span,
As though they held a lion there,
　　And not a fenceless man.
They set him high upon a cart —
　　The hangman rode below —

They drew his hands behind his back,
 And bared his noble brow.
Then, as a hound is slipped from leash,
 They cheered the common throng,
And blew the note with yell and shout,
 And bade him pass along.

It would have made a brave man's heart
 Grow sad and sick that day,
To watch the keen malignant eyes
 Bent down on that array.
There stood the Whig west-country lords
 In balcony and bow,
There sat their gaunt and withered dames,
 And their daughters all a-row.
And every open window
 Was full as full might be
With black-robed Covenanting carles,
 That goodly sport to see !

But when he came, though pale and wan,
 He looked so great and high,
So noble was his manly front,
 So calm his steadfast eye ;—
The rabble rout forbore to shout,
 And each man held his breath,

For well they knew the hero's soul
  Was face to face with death.
And then a mournful shudder
  Through all the people crept,
And some that came to scoff at him
  Now turned aside and wept.

But onwards, always onwards,
  In silence and in gloom,
The dreary pageant labored,
  Till it reached the house of doom.
Then first a woman's voice was heard
  In jeer and laughter loud,
And an angry cry and a hiss arose
  From the heart of the tossing crowd:
Then, as the Græme looked upwards,
  He saw the ugly smile
Of him who sold his king for gold —
  The master-fiend Argyle!

The Marquis gazed a moment,
  And nothing did he say,
But the cheek of Argyle grew ghastly pale,
  And he turned his eyes away.
The painted harlot by his side,
  She shook through every limb,

For a roar like thunder swept the street,
   And hands were clenched at him ;
And a Saxon soldier cried aloud,
   " Back, coward, from thy place !
For seven long years thou hast not dared
   To look him in the face."

Had I been there with sword in hand,
   And fifty Camerons by,
That day through high Dunedin's streets
   Had pealed the slogan-cry.
Not all their troops of trampling horse,
   Nor might of mailèd men —
Not all the rebels in the south
   Had borne us backwards then !
Once more his foot on Highland heath
   Had trod as free as air,
Or I, and all who bore my name,
   Been laid around him there.

It might not be. They placed him next
   Within the solemn hall,
Where once the Scottish kings were throned
   Amidst their nobles all.
But there was dust of vulgar feet
   On that polluted floor,

And perjured traitors filled the place
  Where good men sat before.
With savage glee came Warristoun
  To read the murderous doom ;
And then uprose the great Montrose
  In the middle of the room.

" Now by my faith as belted knight,
  And by the name I bear,
And by the bright Saint Andrew's cross
  That waves above us there —
Yea, by a greater, mightier oath —
  And oh, that such should be ! —
By that dark stream of royal blood
  That lies 'twixt you and me —
I have not sought in battle-field
  A wreath of such renown,
Nor dared I hope on my dying day
  To win the martyr's crown !

" There is a chamber far away
  Where sleep the good and brave,
But a better place ye have named for me
  Than by my father's grave.
For truth and right, 'gainst treason's might,
  This hand hath always striven,

And ye raise it up for a witness still
  In the eye of earth and heaven.
Then nail my head on yonder tower —
  Give every town a limb —
And God who made shall gather them :
  I go from you to Him ! "

The morning dawned full darkly,
  The rain came flashing down,
And the jagged streak of the levin-bolt
  Lit up the gloomy town :
The thunder crashed across the heaven,
  The fatal hour was come ;
Yet aye broke in, with muffled beat,
  The 'larum of the drum.
There was madness on the earth below
  And anger in the sky,
And young and old, and rich and poor,
  Came forth to see him die.

Ah, God ! that ghastly gibbet !
  How dismal 't is to see
The great tall spectral skeleton,
  The ladder and the tree !
Hark ! hark ! it is the clash of arms —
  The bells begin to toll —

" He is coming ! he is coming !
   God's mercy on his soul ! "
One last long peal of thunder —
   The clouds are cleared away,
And the glorious sun once more looks down
   Amidst the dazzling day.

" He is coming ! he is coming ! "
   Like a bridegroom from his room,
Came the hero from his prison
   To the scaffold and the doom.
There was glory on his forehead,
   There was lustre in his eye,
And he never walked to battle
   More proudly than to die ;
There was color in his visage,
   Though the cheeks of all were wan,
And they marvelled as they saw him pass,
   That great and goodly man !

He mounted up the scaffold,
   And he turned him to the crowd ;
But they dared not trust the people,
   So he might not speak aloud.
But he looked upon the heavens,
   And they were clear and blue,

And in the liquid ether
   The eye of God shone through !
Yet a black and murky battlement
   Lay resting on the hill,
As though the thunder slept within —
   All else was calm and still.

The grim Geneva ministers
   With anxious scowl drew near,
As you have seen the ravens flock
   Around the dying deer.
He would not deign them word nor sign,
   But alone he bent the knee,
And veiled his face for Christ's dear grace
   Beneath the gallows-tree.
Then radiant and serene he rose,
   And cast his cloak away ;
For he had ta'en his latest look
   Of earth and sun and day.

A beam of light fell o'er him,
   Like a glory round the shriven,
And he climbed the lofty ladder
   As it were the path to heaven.
Then came a flash from out the cloud,
   And a stunning thunder-roll ;

And no man dared to look aloft,
   For fear was on every soul.
There was another heavy sound,
   A hush and then a groan ;
And darkness swept across the sky —
   The work of death was done !

WILLIAM E. AYTOUN.

Bring the bowl which you boast,
    Fill it up to the brim ;
'T is to him we love most,
    And to all who love him.
Brave gallants, stand up,
    And avaunt, ye base carles !
Were there death in the cup,
    Here 's a health to King Charles !

Though he wanders through dangers,
    Unaided, unknown,
Dependent on strangers,
    Estranged from his own ;
Though 't is under our breath,
    Amidst forfeits and perils,
Here 's to honor and faith,
    And a health to King Charles.

Let such honors abound
   As the time can afford,
The knee on the ground,
   And the hand on the sword ;
But the time shall come round,
   When, mid Lords, Dukes, and Earls,
The loud trumpets shall sound
   Here's a health to King Charles !

Sir Walter Scott, from "Woodstock."

BARCLAY OF URY.

Up the streets of Aberdeen,
By the kirk and college-green,
    Rode the Laird of Ury;
Close behind him, close beside,
Foul of mouth and evil-eyed,
    Pressed the mob in fury.

Flouted him the drunken churl,
Jeered at him the serving-girl,
    Prompt to please her master;
And the begging carlin, late
Fed and clothed at Ury's gate,
    Cursed him as he passed her.

Yet with calm and stately mien,
Up the streets of Aberdeen
    Came he slowly riding;
And, to all he saw and heard,
Answering not with bitter word,
    Turning not for chiding.

Came a troop with broadswords swinging,
Bits and bridles sharply ringing,
    Loose and free and froward ;
Quoth the foremost, " Ride him down !
Push him ! prick him ! through the town
    Drive the Quaker coward ! "

But from out the thickening crowd
Cried a sudden voice and loud :
    " Barclay ! Ho ! a Barclay ! "
And the old man at his side
Saw a comrade, battle-tried,
    Scarred and sunburned darkly, —

Who with ready weapon bare,
Fronting to the troopers there,
    Cried aloud : " God save us !
Call ye coward him who stood
Ankle deep in Lutzen's blood,
    With the brave Gustavus ? "

" Nay, I do not need thy sword,
Comrade mine," said Ury's lord ;
    " Put it up, I pray thee ;
Passive to his holy will,
Trust I in my Master still,
    Even though he slay me.

" Pledges of thy love and faith,
Proved on many a field of death,
    Not by me are needed."
Marvelled much that henchman bold
That his laird, so stout of old,
    Now so meekly pleaded.

" Woe 's the day ! " he sadly said,
With a slowly shaking head,
    And a look of pity ;
" Ury's honest lord reviled,
Mock of knave and sport of child,
    In his own good city !

" Speak the word, and, master mine,
As we charged on Tilly's line,
    And his Walloon lancers,
Smiting through their midst we 'll teach
Civil look and decent speech
    To these boyish prancers ! "

" Marvel not, mine ancient friend,
Like beginning, like the end : "
    Quoth the Laird of Ury,
" Is the sinful servant more
Than his gracious Lord who bore
    Bonds and stripes in Jewry?

" Give me joy that in His name
I can bear, with patient frame,
    All these vain ones offer ;
While for them He suffereth long,
Shall I answer wrong with wrong,
    Scoffing with the scoffer?

" Hâppier I, with loss of all,
Hunted, outlawed, held in thrall,
    With few friends to greet me,
Than when reeve and squire were seen,
Riding out from Aberdeen,
    With bared heads to meet me.

" When each goodwife, o'er and o'er,
Blessed me as I passed her door ;
    And the snooded daughter,
Through her casement glancing down,
Smiled on him who bore renown
    From red fields of slaughter.

" Hard to feel the stranger's scoff,
Hard the old friend's falling off,
    Hard to learn forgiving ;
But the Lord his own rewards,
And his love with theirs accords,
    Warm and fresh and living.

" Through this dark and stormy night
Faith beholds a feeble light
   Up the blackness streaking ;
Knowing God's own time is best,
In a patient hope I rest
   For the full day-breaking ! "

.   .   .   .   .

JOHN GREENLEAF WHITTIER.

THE BONNETS OF BONNY DUNDEE.

1689.

To the Lords of Convention 't was Claver'se who
    spoke,
" Ere the King's crown shall fall there are crowns
    to be broke ;
So let each Cavalier who loves honor and me
Come follow the bonnet of Bonny Dundee ! "

    Come fill up my cup, come fill up my can ;
    Come saddle your horses, and call up your men ;
    Come open the West Port and let me gang free,
    And it's room for the bonnets of Bonny Dundee !

Dundee he is mounted, he rides up the street,
The bells are rung backward, the drums they are
    beat ;
But the Provost, douce man, said, " Just e'en let
    him be,
The gude toun is weel quit of that deil of Dundee ! "

    Come fill up my cup, &c.

As he rode down the sanctified bends of the
    Bow,
Ilk carline was flyting and shaking her pow ;
But the young plants of grace they looked couthie
    and slee,
Thinking, " Luck to thy bonnet, thou Bonny
    Dundee."

       Come fill up my cup, &c.

With sour-featured Whigs the Grass-market was
    crammed,
As if half the West had set tryst to be hanged ;
There was spite in each look, there was fear in
    each e'e,
As they watched for the bonnets of Bonny Dundee.

       Come fill up my cup, &c.

These cowls of Kilmarnock had spits and had
    spears,
And lang-hafted gullies to kill Cavaliers ;
But they shrunk to close-heads, and the causeway
    was free
At the toss of the bonnet of Bonny Dundee.

       Come fill up my cup, &c.

He spurred to the foot of the proud Castle rock,
And with the gay Gordon he gallantly spoke :
" Let Mons Meg and her marrows speak twa words
    or three,
For the love of the bonnet of Bonny Dundee."

      Come fill up my cup, &c.

The Gordon demands of him which way he
    goes, —
" Where'er shall direct me the shade of Montrose !
Your grace in short time shall hear tidings of
    me,
Or that low lies the bonnet of Bonny Dundee."

      Come fill up my cup, &c.

" There are hills beyond Pentland and lands
    beyond Forth ;
If there 's lords in the Lowlands, there 's chiefs in
    the North ;
There are wild Duniewassals three thousand times
    three
Will cry *Hoigh !* for the bonnet of Bonny
    Dundee."

      Come fill up my cup, &c.

" There 's brass on the target of darkened bull-hide,
There 's steel in the scabbard that dangles beside ;
The brass shall be burnished, the steel shall flash
    free,
At a toss of the bonnet of Bonny Dundee."

      Come fill up my cup, &c.

" Away to the hills, to the caves, to the rocks ;
Ere I own a usurper, I 'll couch with the fox ;
And tremble, false Whigs, in the midst of your glee,
You have not seen the last of my bonnet and me ! "

      Come fill up my cup, &c.

He waved his proud hand, and the trumpets were
    blown,
The kettle-drums clashed and the horsemen rode on,
Till on Ravelston's cliffs and on Clermiston's lea
Died away the wild war-notes of Bonny Dundee.

    Come fill up my cup, come fill up my can ;
    Come saddle the horses, and call up the men ;
    Come open your gates, and let me gae free,
      For it 's up with the bonnets of Bonny
      Dundee !

                  Sir Walter Scott.

THE BURIAL-MARCH OF DUNDEE.

JULY, 1689.

SOUND the fife, and cry the slogan —
    Let the pibroch shake the air
With its wild triumphal music,
    Worthy of the freight we bear.
Let the ancient hills of Scotland
    Hear once more the battle-song
Swell within their glens and valleys
    As the clansmen march along !
Never from the field of combat,
    Never from the deadly fray,
Was a nobler trophy carried
    Than we bring with us to-day ;
Never since the valiant Douglas
    On his dauntless bosom bore
Good King Robert's heart — the priceless —
    To our dear Redeemer's shore !
Lo ! we bring with us the hero —
    Lo ! we bring the conquering Græme,
Crowned as best beseems a victor
    From the altar of his fame ;

Fresh and bleeding from the battle
   Whence his spirit took its flight,
Midst the crashing charge of squadrons,
   And the thunder of the fight !
Strike, I say, the notes of triumph,
   As we march o'er moor and lea !
Is there any here will venture
   To bewail our dead Dundee?
Let the widows of the traitors
   Weep until their eyes are dim !
Wail ye may full well for Scotland —
   Let none dare to mourn for him !
See ! above his glorious body
   Lies the royal banner's fold —
See ! his valiant blood is mingled
   With its crimson and its gold —
See how calm he looks, and stately,
   Like a warrior on his shield,
Waiting till the flush of morning
   Breaks along the battle-field !
See — oh never more, my comrades,
   Shall we see that falcon eye
Redden with its inward lightning,
   As the hour of fight drew nigh !
Never shall we hear the voice that,
   Clearer than the trumpet's call,
Bade us strike for king and country,
   Bade us win the field, or fall !

On the heights of Killiecrankie
    Yester-morn our army lay ;
Slowly rose the mist in columns
    From the river's broken way ;
Hoarsely roared the swollen torrent,
    And the Pass was wrapped in gloom,
When the clansmen rose together
    From their lair amidst the broom.
Then we belted on our tartans,
    And our bonnets down we drew,
And we felt our broadswords' edges,
    And we proved them to be true ;
And we prayed the prayer of soldiers,
    And we cried the gathering-cry,
And we clasped the hands of kinsmen,
    And we swore to do or die !
Then our leader rode before us
    On his war-horse black as night —
Well the Cameronian rebels
    Knew that charger in the fight ! —
And a cry of exultation
    From the bearded warriors rose ;
For we loved the house of Claver'se,
    And we thought of good Montrose.
But he raised his hand for silence —
    "Soldiers ! I have sworn a vow :
Ere the evening star shall glisten
    On Schehallion's lofty brow,

Either we shall rest in triumph,
   Or another of the Græmes
Shall have died in battle-harness
   For his country and King James !
Think upon the Royal Martyr —
   Think of what his race endure ;
Think on him whom butchers murdered
   On the field of Magus Muir : —
By his sacred blood I charge ye,
   By the ruined hearth and shrine —
By the blighted hopes of Scotland,
   By your injuries and mine —
Strike this day as if the anvil
   Lay beneath your blows the while,
Be they Covenanting traitors,
   Or the brood of false Argyle !
Strike ! and drive the trembling rebels
   Backwards o'er the stormy Forth ;
Let them tell their pale Convention
   How they fared within the North.
Let them tell that Highland honor
   Is not to be bought nor sold,
That we scorn their prince's anger
   As we loathe his foreign gold.
Strike ! and when the fight is over,
   If you look in vain for me,
Where the dead are lying thickest
   Search for him that was Dundee !"

Loudly then the hills re-echoed
   With our answer to his call,
But a deeper echo sounded
   In the bosoms of us all.
For the lands of wide Breadalbane,
   Not a man who heard him speak
Would that day have left the battle.
   Burning eye and flushing cheek
Told the clansmen's fierce emotion,
   And they harder drew their breath ;
For their souls were strong within them,
   Stronger than the grasp of death.
Soon we heard a challenge-trumpet
   Sounding in the Pass below,
And the distant tramp of horses,
   And the voices of the foe ;
Down we crouched amid the bracken,
   Till the Lowland ranks drew near,
Panting like the hounds in summer,
   When they scent the stately deer.
From the dark defile emerging,
   Next we saw the squadrons come,
Leslie's foot and Leven's troopers
   Marching to the tuck of drum ;
Through the scattered wood of birches,
   O'er the broken ground and heath,
Wound the long battalion slowly,
   Till they gained the field beneath ;

Then we bounded from our covert,—
    Judge how looked the Saxons then,
When they saw the rugged mountain
    Start to life with armèd men !
Like a tempest down the ridges
    Swept the hurricane of steel,
Rose the slogan of Macdonald —
    Flashed the broadsword of Locheill !
Vainly sped the withering volley
    'Mongst the foremost of our band —
On we poured until we met them,
    Foot to foot, and hand to hand.
Horse and man went down like driftwood
    When the floods are black at Yule,
And their carcasses are whirling
    In the Garry's deepest pool.
Horse and man went down before us —
    Living foe there tarried none
On the field of Killiecrankie,
    When that stubborn fight was done !

And the evening star was shining
    On Schehallion's distant head,
When we wiped our bloody broadswords
    And returned to count the dead.
There we found him gashed and gory,
    Stretched upon the cumbered plain,

As he told us where to seek him,
  In the thickest of the slain.
And a smile was on his visage,
  For within his dying ear
Pealed the joyful note of triumph,
  And the clansmen's clamorous cheer;
So, amidst the battle's thunder,
  Shot, and steel, and scorching flame,
In the glory of his manhood
  Passed the spirit of the Græme !

Open wide the vaults of Athol,
  Where the bones of heroes rest —
Open wide the hallowed portals
  To receive another guest !
Last of Scots, and last of freemen —
  Last of all that dauntless race
Who would rather die unsullied
  Than outlive the land's disgrace !
O thou lion-hearted warrior !
  Reck not of the after-time :
Honor may be deemed dishonor,
  Loyalty be called a crime.
Sleep in peace with kindred ashes
  Of the noble and the true,
Hands that never failed their country,
  Hearts that never baseness knew.

Sleep ! — and till the latest trumpet
   Wakes the dead from earth and sea,
Scotland shall not boast a braver
   Chieftain than our own Dundee !

WILLIAM E. AYTOUN.

" It was a' for our rightfu' king
    We left fair Scotland's strand !
It was a' for our rightfu' king
    We e'er saw Irish land, my dear,
    We e'er saw Irish land.

" Now a' is done that men can do,
    An' a' is done in vain :
My love an' native land, farewell,
    For I maun cross the main, my dear,
    For I maun cross the main."

He turned him right an' round about,
    Upon the Irish shore,
An' ga'e his bridle-reins a shake,
    With, " Adieu for evermore, my dear,"
    With, " Adieu for evermore."

The sodger frae the wars returns,
  The sailor frae the main ;
But I hae parted frae my love,
  Never to meet again, my dear,
  Never to meet again.

When day is gane, and night is come,
  An' a' folk bound to sleep,
I think on him that 's far awa',
  The lee-lang night, an' weep, my dear,
  The lee-lang night, an' weep.

This song is traditionally said to have been written by a Captain Ogilvie, related to the house of Inverquharity, who was with King James II. in his Irish expedition, and was in the battle of the Boyne, in 1690. He was a brave man, and fell in an engagement on the Rhine.

THE ISLAND OF THE SCOTS.

1697.

THE Rhine is running deep and red,
   The island lies before —
" Now is there one of all the host
   Will dare to venture o'er?
For not alone the river's sweep
   Might make a brave man quail ;
The foe are on the further side,
   Their shot comes fast as hail.
God help us, if the middle isle
   We may not hope to win !
Now is there any of the host
   Will dare to venture in ? "

" The ford is deep, the banks are steep,
   The island-shore lies wide ;
Nor man nor horse could stem its force,
   Or reach the further side.
See there ! amidst the willow-boughs
   The serried bayonets gleam ;

They 've flung their bridge, they 've
    won the isle ;
  The foes have crossed the stream !
Their volley flashes sharp and strong, —
    By all the saints ! I trow
There never yet was soldier born
    Could force that passage now ! "

So spoke the bold French Mareschal
    With him who led the van,
Whilst rough and red before their view
    The turbid river ran.
Nor bridge nor boat had they to cross
    The wild and swollen Rhine,
And thundering on the other bank
    Far stretched the German line.
Hard by there stood a swarthy man
    Was leaning on his sword,
And a saddened smile lit up his face
    As he heard the Captain's word.
" I 've seen a wilder stream ere now
    Than that which rushes there ;
I 've stemmed a heavier torrent yet
    And never thought to dare.
If German steel be sharp and keen,
    Is ours not strong and true?
There may be danger in the deed,
    But there is honor too."

The old lord in his saddle turned,
   And hastily he said —
" Hath bold Duguesclin's fiery heart
   Awakened from the dead ?
Thou art the leader of the Scots —
   Now well and sure I know,
That gentle blood in dangerous hour
   Ne'er yet ran cold nor slow.
And I have seen ye in the fight
   Do all that mortal may :
If honor is the boon ye seek,
   It may be won this day.
The prize is in the middle isle,
   There lies the adventurous way,
And armies twain are on the plain,
   The daring deed to see —
Now ask thy gallant company
   If they will follow thee ! "

Right gladsome looked the Captain then,
   And nothing did he say,
But he turned him to his little band —
   Oh, few I ween, were they !
The relics of the bravest force
   That ever fought in fray.
No one of all that company
   But bore a gentle name,
Not one whose fathers had not stood
   In Scotland's fields of fame.

All they had marched with great Dundee
   To where he fought and fell,
And in the deadly battle-strife
   Had venged their leader well ;
And they had bent the knee to earth
   When every eye was dim,   .
As o'er their hero's buried corpse
   They sang the funeral hymn ;
And they had trod the Pass once more,
   And stooped on either side
To pluck the heather from the spot
   Where he had dropped and died ;
And they had bound it next their hearts,
   And ta'en a last farewell
Of Scottish earth and Scottish sky,
   Where Scotland's glory fell.
Then went they forth to foreign lands
   Like bent and broken men,
Who leave their dearest hope behind,
   And may not turn again.

"The stream," he said, " is broad and deep,
   And stubborn is the foe ;
Yon island-strength is guarded well—
   Say, brothers, will ye go?
From home and kin for many a year
   Our steps have wandered wide,
And never may our bones be laid
   Our fathers' graves beside.

No children have we to lament,
　　No wives to wail our fall ;
The traitor's and the spoiler's hand
　　Have reft our hearths of all.
But we have hearts, and we have arms,
　　As strong to will and dare
As when our ancient banners flew
　　Within the northern air.
Come, brothers ! let me name a spell
　　Shall rouse your souls again,
And send the old blood bounding free
　　Through pulse, and heart, and vein.
Call back the days of bygone years —
　　Be young and strong once more ;
Think yonder stream, so stark and red,
　　Is one we 've crossed before.
Rise, hill and glen ! rise, crag and wood !
　　Rise up on either hand —
Again upon the Garry's banks,
　　On Scottish soil we stand !
Again I see the tartans wave,
　　Again the trumpets ring ;
Again I hear our leader's call —
　　'Upon them for the King !'
Stayed we behind that glorious day
　　For roaring flood or linn?
The soul of Græme is with us still —
　　Now, brothers ! will ye in ? "

No stay — no pause.   With one accord
   They grasped each other's hand,
And plunged into the angry flood,
   That bold and dauntless band.
High flew the spray above their heads,
   Yet onward still they bore,
Midst cheer, and shout, and answering yell,
   And shot, and cannon-roar.
" Now by the Holy Cross ! I swear,
   Since earth and sea began
Was never such a daring deed
   Essayed by mortal man ! "

Thick blew the smoke across the stream,
   And faster flashed the flame ;
The water plashed in hissing jets
   As ball and bullet came.
Yet onwards pushed the Cavaliers,
   All stern and undismayed,
With thousand armèd foes before,
   And none behind to aid.
Once, as they neared the middle stream,
   So strong the current swept,
That scarce that long and living wall
   Their dangerous footing kept.
Then rose a warning cry behind,
   A joyous shout before :

" The current 's strong, the way is long —
  They 'll never reach the shore !
See ! see ! they stagger in the midst,
  They waver in their line !
Fire on the madmen ! break their ranks
  And whelm them in the Rhine ! "

Have you seen the tall trees swaying
  When the blast is piping shrill,
And the whirlwind reels in fury
  Down the gorges of the hill?
How they toss their mighty branches,
  Striving with the tempest's shock ;
How they keep their place of vantage,
  Cleaving firmly to the rock?
Even so the Scottish warriors
  Held their own against the river ;
Though the water flashed around them,
  Not an eye was seen to quiver !
Though the shot flew sharp and deadly,
  Not a man relaxed his hold ;
For their hearts were big and thrilling
  With the mighty thoughts of old.
One word was spoke among them,
  And through the ranks it spread : —
" Remember our dead Claverhouse ! "
  Was all the Captain said.

Then, sternly bending forward,
    They struggled on awhile,
Until they cleared the heavy stream,
    Then rushèd towards the isle.

The German heart is stout and true,
    The German arm is strong;
The German foot goes seldom back
    Where armèd foemen throng.
But never had they faced in field
    So stern a charge before,
And never had they felt the sweep
    Of Scotland's broad claymore.
Not fiercer pours the avalanche
    Adown the steep incline,
That rises o'er the parent-springs
    Of rough and rapid Rhine;
Scarce swifter shoots the bolt from heaven
    Than came the Scottish band,
Right up against the guarded trench,
    And o'er it sword in hand.
In vain their leaders forward press —
    They meet the deadly brand.

O lonely island of the Rhine,
    Where seed was never sown,
What harvest lay upon thy sands,
    By those strong reapers thrown?

What saw the winter moon that night,
  As, struggling through the rain,
She poured a wan and fitful light
  On marsh, and stream, and plain?
A dreary spot with corpses strewn,
  And bayonets glistening round;
A broken bridge, a stranded boat,
  A bare and battered mound;
And one huge watch-fire's kindled pile,
  That sent its quivering glare
To tell the leaders of the host
  The conquering Scots were there!

And did they twine the laurel-wreath
  For those who fought so well?
And did they honor those who lived,
  And weep for those who fell?
What meed of thanks was given to them
  Let agèd annals tell.
Why should they twine the laurel-wreath, —
  Why crown the cup with wine?
It was not Frenchmen's blood that flowed
  So freely on the Rhine;
A stranger band of beggared men
  Had done the venturous deed:
The glory was to France alone,
  The danger was their meed.

And what cared they for idle thanks
    From foreign prince and peer?
What virtue had such honeyed words
    The exiled heart to cheer?
What mattered it that men should vaunt,
    And loud and fondly swear,
That higher feat of chivalry
    Was never wrought elsewhere?
They bore within their breasts the grief
    That fame can never heal —
The deep, unutterable woe
    Which none save exiles feel.
Their hearts were yearning for the land
    They ne'er might see again —
For Scotland's high and heathered hills,
    For mountain, loch, and glen —
For those who haply lay at rest
    Beyond the distant sea,
Beneath the green and daisied turf
    Where they would gladly be !

Long years went by.   The lonely isle
    In Rhine's impetuous flood
Has ta'en another name from those
    Who bought it with their blood ;
And, though the legend does not live,
    For legends lightly die,

The peasant, as he sees the stream
   In winter rolling by,
And foaming o'er its channel-bed
   Between him and the spot
Won by the warriors of the sword,
Still calls that deep and dangerous ford
   The Passage of the Scot.

WILLIAM E. AYTOUN.

PAUL REVERE'S RIDE.

LISTEN, my children, and you shall hear
Of the midnight ride of Paul Revere,
On the eighteenth of April, in Seventy-five;
Hardly a man is now alive
Who remembers that famous day and year.

He said to his friend, " If the British march
By land or sea from the town to-night,
Hang a lantern aloft in the belfry-arch
Of the North Church tower as a signal-light, —
One, if by land, and two, if by sea;
And I on the opposite shore will be,
Ready to ride and spread the alarm
Through every Middlesex village and farm,
For the country folk to be up and to arm."

Then he said, "Good-night!" and with muffled oar
Silently rowed to the Charlestown shore,
Just as the moon rose over the bay,
Where swinging wide at her moorings lay
The Somerset, British man-of-war;
A phantom ship, with each mast and spar
Across the moon like a prison bar,
And a huge black hulk, that was magnified
By its own reflection in the tide.

Meanwhile, his friend, through alley and street,
Wanders and watches with eager ears,
Till in the silence around him he hears
The muster of men at the barrack door,
The sound of arms, and the tramp of feet,
And the measured tread of the grenadiers,
Marching down to their boats on the shore.

Then he climbed the tower of the old North Church,
By the wooden stairs, with stealthy tread,
To the belfry-chamber overhead,
And startled the pigeons from their perch
On the sombre rafters, that round him made
Masses and moving shapes of shade, —
By the trembling ladder, steep and tall,
To the highest window in the wall,
Where he paused to listen and look down
A moment on the roofs of the town,
And the moonlight flowing over all.

Beneath, in the churchyard, lay the dead,
In their night-encampment on the hill,
Wrapped in silence so deep and still
That he could hear, like a sentinel's tread,
The watchful night-wind, as it went
Creeping along from tent to tent,
And seeming to whisper, " All is well ! "
A moment only he feels the spell
Of the place and the hour, and the secret dread
Of the lonely belfry and the dead ;
For suddenly all his thoughts are bent
On a shadowy something far away,
Where the river widens to meet the bay, —
A line of black that bends and floats
On the rising tide, like a bridge of boats.

Meanwhile, impatient to mount and ride,
Booted and spurred, with a heavy stride,
On the opposite shore walked Paul Revere.
Now he patted his horse's side,
Now gazed at the landscape far and near,
Then, impetuous, stamped the earth
And turned and tightened his saddle-girth ;
But mostly he watched with eager search
The belfry-tower of the old North Church,
As it rose above the graves on the hill,
Lonely and spectral and sombre and still.
And lo ! as he looks, on the belfry's height

A glimmer, and then a gleam of light !
He springs to the saddle, the bridle he turns,
But lingers and gazes, till full on his sight
A second lamp in the belfry burns !

A hurry of hoofs in a village street,
A shape in the moonlight, a bulk in the dark,
And beneath, from the pebbles in passing, a spark
Struck out by a steed flying fearless and fleet :
That was all !   And yet through the gloom and the
    light,
The fate of a nation was riding that night ;
And the spark struck out by that steed, in his flight,
Kindled the land into flame with its heat.

He has left the village and mounted the steep,
And beneath him, tranquil and broad and deep,
Is the Mystic, meeting the ocean tides ;
And under the alders, that skirt its edge,
Now soft on the sand, now loud on the ledge,
Is heard the tramp of his steed as he rides.

It was twelve by the village clock
When he crossed the bridge into Medford town.
He heard the crowing of the cock,
And the barking of the farmer's dog,
And felt the damp of the river fog,
That rises after the sun goes down.

It was one by the village clock,
When he galloped into Lexington.
He saw the gilded weathercock
Swim in the moonlight as he passed,
And the meeting-house windows, blank and bare,
Gaze at him with a spectral glare,
As if they already stood aghast
At the bloody work they would look upon.

It was two by the village clock
When he came to the bridge in Concord town.
He heard the bleating of the flock,
And the twitter of birds among the trees,
And felt the breath of the morning breeze
Blowing over the meadows brown.
And one was safe and asleep in his bed
Who at the bridge would be first to fall,
Who that day would be lying dead,
Pierced by a British musket-ball.

You know the rest.   In the books you have read,
How the British Regulars fired and fled, —
How the farmers gave them ball for ball,
From behind each fence and farm-yard wall,
Chasing the red-coats down the lane,
Then crossing the fields to emerge again
Under the trees at the turn of the road,
And only pausing to fire and load.

So through the night rode Paul Revere ;
And so through the night went his cry of alarm
To every Middlesex village and farm, —
A cry of defiance and not of fear,
A voice in the darkness, a knock at the door,
And a word that shall echo forevermore !
For, borne on the night-wind of the past,
Through all our history, to the last,
In the hour of darkness and peril and need,
The people will waken and listen to hear
The hurrying hoof-beats of that steed,
And the midnight message of Paul Revere.

HENRY W. LONGFELLOW.

SONG OF MARION'S MEN.

1780 – 1781

Our band is few, but true and tried,
  Our leader frank and bold;
The British soldier trembles
  When Marion's name is told.
Our fortress is the good greenwood,
  Our tent the cypress-tree;
We know the forest round us,
  As seamen know the sea;
We know its walks of thorny vines,
  Its glades of reedy grass,
Its safe and silent islands
  Within the dark morass.

Woe to the English soldiery
  That little dread us near!
On them shall light at midnight
  A strange and sudden fear;
When, waking to their tents on fire,
  They grasp their arms in vain,

And they who stand to face us
　Are beat to earth again ;
And they who fly in terror deem
　A mighty host behind,
And hear the tramp of thousands
　Upon the hollow wind.

Then sweet the hour that brings release
　From danger and from toil ;
We talk the battle over,
　And share the battle's spoil.
The woodland rings with laugh and shout,
　As if a hunt were up,
And woodland flowers are gathered
　To crown the soldier's cup.
With merry songs we mock the wind
　That in the pine-top grieves,
And slumber long and sweetly
　On beds of oaken leaves.

Well knows the fair and friendly moon
　The band that Marion leads —
The glitter of their rifles,
　The scampering of their steeds.
'T is life to guide the fiery barb
　Across the moonlight plain ;
'T is life to feel the night-wind
　That lifts his tossing mane.

A moment in the British camp —
   A moment — and away,
Back to the pathless forest,
   Before the peep of day.

Grave men there are by broad Santee,
   Grave men with hoary hairs ;
Their hearts are all with Marion,
   For Marion are their prayers.
And lovely ladies greet our band,
   With kindest welcoming,
With smiles like those of summer,
   And tears like those of spring.
For them we wear these trusty arms,
   And lay them down no more
Till we have driven the Briton,
   Forever, from our shore.

                WILLIAM CULLEN BRYANT.

THE BATTLE OF THE BALTIC.

APRIL 2, 1801.

OF Nelson and the North,
Sing the glorious day's renown,
When to battle fierce came forth
All the might of Denmark's crown,
And her arms along the deep proudly shone ;
By each gun the lighted brand,
In a bold determined hand,
And the Prince of all the land
Led them on.

Like leviathans afloat,
Lay their bulwarks on the brine ;
While the sign of battle flew
On the lofty British line ;
It was ten of April morn by the chime :
As they drifted on their path,
There was silence deep as death ;
And the boldest held his breath,
For a time.

But the might of England flushed
To anticipate the scene ;
And her van the fleeter rushed
O'er the deadly space between.
" Hearts of oak ! " our captains cried, when each
     gun
From its adamantine lips
Spread a death-shade round the ships,
Like the hurricane eclipse
Of the sun.

Again ! again ! again !
And the havoc did not slack,
Till a feeble cheer the Dane
To our cheering sent us back ;
Their shots along the deep slowly boom ;
Then ceased — and all is wail,
As they strike the shattered sail,
Or, in conflagration pale,
Light the gloom.

Out spoke the victor then,
As he hailed them o'er the wave :
" Ye are brothers ! ye are men !
And we conquer but to save,—
So peace instead of death let us bring ;

But yield, proud foe, thy fleet,
With the crews, at England's feet,
And make submission meet
To our King "

Then Denmark blest our chief,
That he gave her wounds repose ;
And the sounds of joy and grief
From her people wildly rose,
As death withdrew his shades from the day.
While the sun looked smiling bright
O'er a wide and woful sight,
Where the fires of funeral light
Died away.

Now joy, old England, raise !
For the tidings of thy might,
By the festal cities' blaze,
While the wine-cup shines in light ;
And yet amidst that joy and uproar,
Let us think of them that sleep,
Full many a fathom deep,
By thy wild and stormy steep,
Elsinore !

Brave hearts ! to Britain's pride
Once so faithful and so true,
On the deck of fame that died,

With the gallant good Riou ;
Soft sigh the winds of Heaven o'er their grave !
While the billow mournful rolls,
And the mermaid's song condoles,
Singing glory to the souls
Of the brave !

THOMAS CAMPBELL.

YE MARINERS OF ENGLAND.

Ye Mariners of England !
That guard our native seas ;
Whose flag has braved a thousand years
The battle and the breeze !
Your glorious standard launch again
To match another foe !
And sweep through the deep,
While the stormy winds do blow ;
While the battle rages loud and long,
And the stormy winds do blow.

The spirits of your fathers
Shall start from every wave ! —
For the deck it was their field of fame,
And Ocean was their grave :
Where Blake and mighty Nelson fell,
Your manly hearts shall glow,
As ye sweep through the deep,
While the stormy winds do blow ;
While the battle rages loud and long,
And the stormy winds do blow.

Britannia needs no bulwarks,
No towers along the steep ;
Her march is o'er the mountain-waves,
Her home is on the deep.
With thunders from her native oak,
She quells the floods below, —
As they roar on the shore,
When the stormy winds do blow ;
When the battle rages loud and long,
And the stormy winds do blow.

The meteor flag of England
Shall yet terrific burn ;
Till danger's troubled night depart,
And the star of peace return.
Then, then, ye ocean-warriors !
Our song and feast shall flow
To the fame of your name,
When the storm has ceased to blow ;
When the fiery fight is heard no more,
And the storm has ceased to blow.

THOMAS CAMPBELL.

INCIDENT OF THE FRENCH CAMP.

You know, we French stormed Ratisbon :
   A mile or so away,
On a little mound, Napoleon
   Stood, on our storming-day ;
With neck thrust out, you fancy how,
   Legs wide, arms locked behind,
As if to balance the prone brow
   Oppressive with its mind.

Just as perhaps he mused : " My plans
   That soar, to earth may fall,
Let once my army-leader Lannes
   Waver at yonder wall, " —
Out 'twixt the battery-smokes there flew
   A rider, bound on bound
Full-galloping ; nor bridle drew
   Until he reached the mound.

Then off there flung in smiling joy,
   And held himself erect
By just his horse's mane, a boy :
   You hardly could suspect —

(So tight he kept his lips compressed,
  Scarce any blood came through)
You looked twice ere you saw his breast
  Was all but shot in two.

" Well," cried he, " Emperor, by God's grace
  We 've got you Ratisbon !
The Marshal 's in the market-place,
  And you 'll be there anon
To see your flag-bird flap his vans
  Where I, to heart's desire,
Perched him !" The Chief's eye flashed ; his plans
  Soared up again like fire.

The Chief's eye flashed ; but presently
  Softened itself, as sheathes
A film the mother-eagle's eye
  When her bruised eaglet breathes ;
" You 're wounded !" " Nay," his soldier's pride
  Touched to the quick, he said :
" I 'm killed, Sire !" And, his chief beside,
  Smiling the boy fell dead.

ROBERT BROWNING.

THE BURIAL OF SIR JOHN MOORE.

1809.

Not a drum was heard, not a funeral note,
   As his corse to the rampart we hurried;
Not a soldier discharged his farewell shot
   O'er the grave where our hero we buried.

We buried him darkly at dead of night,
   The sod with our bayonets turning;
By the struggling moonbeam's misty light,
   And the lantern dimly burning.

No useless coffin enclosed his breast,
   Not in sheet nor in shroud we wound him;
But he lay like a warrior taking his rest,
   With his martial cloak around him!

Few and short were the prayers we said,
   And we spoke not a word of sorrow;
But we steadfastly gazed on the face that was dead,
   And we bitterly thought of the morrow.

We thought, as we hollowed his narrow bed,
　And smoothed down his lonely pillow,
That the foe and the stranger would tread o'er his
　　　head,
　And we far away on the billow !

Lightly they 'll talk of the spirit that 's gone,
　And o'er his cold ashes upbraid him ;
But little he 'll reck if they let him sleep on,
　In the grave where a Briton has laid him.

But half of our heavy task was done,
　When the clock struck the hour for retiring ;
And we heard the distant random gun
　That the foe was sullenly firing.

Slowly and sadly we laid him down,
　From the field of his fame fresh and gory ;
We carved not a line, and we raised not a stone —
　But we left him alone with his glory !

CHARLES WOLFE.

MARCO BOZZARIS.

AUGUST 20, 1823.

AT midnight, in his guarded tent,
   The Turk was dreaming of the hour
When Greece, her knee in suppliance bent,
   Should tremble at his power :
In dreams, through camp and court, he bore
The trophies of a conqueror ;
   In dreams his song of triumph heard ;
Then wore his monarch's signet-ring :
Then pressed that monarch's throne — a king ;
As wild his thoughts, and gay of wing,
   As Eden's garden bird.

At midnight, in the forest shades,
   Bozzaris ranged his Suliote band,
True as the steel of their tried blades,
   Heroes in heart and hand.

There had the Persian's thousands stood,
There had the glad earth drunk their blood
　　On old Platæa's day ;
And now there breathed that haunted air
The sons of sires who conquered there,
With arm to strike, and soul to dare,
　　As quick, as far, as they.

An hour passed on — the Turk awoke ;
　　That bright dream was his last ;
He woke — to hear his sentries shriek,
　　"To arms ! they come ! the Greek ! the Greek !"
He woke — to die midst flame, and smoke,
And shout, and groan, and sabre-stroke,
　　And death-shots falling thick and fast
As lightnings from the mountain-cloud ;
And heard, with voice as trumpet loud,
　　Bozzaris cheer his band :
" Strike — till the last armed foe expires ;
Strike — for your altars and your fires ;
Strike — for the green graves of your sires ;
　　God — and your native land !"

They fought — like brave men, long and well ;
　　They piled that ground with Moslem slain ;
They conquered — but Bozzaris fell,
　　Bleeding at every vein.

His few surviving comrades saw
His smile when rang their proud *hurrah*,
   And the red field was won ;
Then saw in death his eyelids close
Calmly, as to a night's repose,
   Like flowers at set of sun.

Come to the bridal-chamber, Death !
   Come to the mother's, when she feels,
For the first time, her first-born's breath ;
   Come when the blessèd seals
That close the pestilence are broke,
   And crowded cities wail its stroke ;
Come in consumption's ghastly form,
The earthquake shock, the ocean-storm ;
Come when the heart beats high and warm,
   With banquet-song, and dance, and wine ;
And thou art terrible — the tear,
The groan, the knell, the pall, the bier,
And all we know, or dream, or fear,
   Of agony, are thine.

But to the hero, when his sword
   Has won the battle for the free,
Thy voice sounds like a prophet's word ;
And in its hollow tones are heard
   The thanks of millions yet to be.

Come, when his task of fame is wrought —
Come, with her laurel-leaf, blood-bought —
   Come in her crowning hour — and then
Thy sunken eye's unearthly light
To him is welcome as the sight
   Of sky and stars to prisoned men ;
Thy grasp is welcome as the hand
Of brother in a foreign land ;
Thy summons welcome as the cry
That told the Indian isles were nigh
   To the world-seeking Genoese,
When the land-wind, from woods of palm,
And orange-groves, and fields of balm,
   Blew o'er the Haytian seas.

Bozzaris ! with the storied brave
   Greece nurtured in her glory's time,
Rest thee — there is no prouder grave,
   Even in her own proud clime.
She wore no funeral weeds for thee,
   Nor bade the dark hearse wave its plume,
Like torn branch from death's leafless tree,
In sorrow's pomp and pageantry,
   The heartless luxury of the tomb :
But she remembers thee as one
Long-loved, and for a season gone ;
For thee her poet's lyre is wreathed,
Her marble wrought, her music breathed ;

For thee she rings the birthday bells ;
Of thee her babes' first lisping tells ;
For thine her evening prayer is said
At palace-couch, and cottage-bed ;
Her soldier, closing with the foe,
Gives for thy sake a deadlier blow ;
His plighted maiden, when she fears
For him, the joy of her young years,
Thinks of thy fate, and checks her tears ;
  And she, the mother of thy boys,
Though in her eye and faded cheek
Is read the grief she will not speak,
  The memory of her buried joys —
And even she who gave thee birth,
Will, by their pilgrim-circled hearth,
  Talk of thy doom without a sigh ;
For thou art Freedom's now, and Fame's —
One of the few, the immortal names
  That were not born to die.

FITZ-GREENE HALLECK.

OLD IRONSIDES.

Ay, tear her tattered ensign down !
   Long has it waved on high,
And many an eye has danced to see
   That banner in the sky ;
Beneath it rung the battle shout,
   And burst the cannon's roar, —
The meteor of the ocean air
   Shall sweep the clouds no more !

Her deck, once red with heroes' blood,
   Where knelt the vanquished foe,
When winds were hurrying o'er the flood,
   And waves were white below,
No more shall feel the victor's tread,
   Or know the conquered knee ;
The harpies of the shore shall pluck
   The eagle of the sea !

O better that her shattered hulk
  Should sink beneath the wave ;
Her thunders shook the mighty deep,
  And there should be her grave ;
Nail to the mast her holy flag,
  Set every threadbare sail,
And give her to the god of storms,
  The lightning and the gale !

OLIVER WENDELL HOLMES.

THE RED THREAD OF HONOR.

A.D. 1845.

Told to the Author by the late General Sir
Charles James Napier.

Eleven men of England
A breastwork charged in vain;
Eleven men of England
Lie stripped, and gashed, and slain.
Slain; but of foes that guarded
Their rock-built fortress well,
Some twenty had been mastered,
When the last soldier fell.

Whilst Napier piloted his wondrous way
Across the sand-waves of the desert-sea;
Then flashed at once, on each fierce clan, dismay,
Lord of their wild Truckee.[1]

[1] A stronghold in the Desert, supposed to be inaccessible
and impregnable.

These missed the glen to which their steps were
    bent,
Mistook a mandate, from afar half heard,
And, in that glorious error, calmly went
        To death without a word.

        The robber-chief mused deeply,
        Above those daring dead ;
        " Bring here," at length he shouted,
        " Bring quick, the battle-thread.
        Let Eblis blast forever
        Their souls, if Allah will,
        But WE must keep unbroken
        The old rules of the Hill.

        " Before the Ghiznee tiger
        Leapt forth to burn and slay ;
        Before the holy Prophet
        Taught our grim tribes to pray ;
        Before Secunder's [1] lances
        Pierced through each Indian glen, —
        The mountain laws of honor
        Were framed for fearless men.

        [1] Alexander.

" Still, when a chief dies bravely,
We bind with green *one* wrist, —
Green for the brave ; for heroes
ONE crimson thread we twist.
Say ye, O gallant Hillmen,
For these whose life has fled,
Which is the fitting color,
The green one, or the red ? "

" Our brethren, laid in honored graves, may wear
Their green reward," each noble savage said ;
" To these, whom hawks and hungry wolves shall
        tear,
    Who dares deny the red ? "

Thus conquering hate, and steadfast to the right,
Fresh from the heart that haughty verdict came ;
Beneath a waning moon each spectral height
    Rolled back its loud acclaim.

Once more the chief gazed keenly
Down on those daring dead ;
From his good sword their heart's blood
Crept to that crimson thread.
Once more he cried : " The judgment,

Good friends, is wise and true ;
But though the red be given,
Have we not more to do ?

"These were not stirred by anger,
Nor yet by lust made bold ;
Renown they thought above them,
Nor did they look for gold.
To them their leader's signal
Was as the voice of God ;
Unmoved, and uncomplaining,
The path it showed, they trod.

" As, without sound or struggle,
The stars unhurrying march,
Where Allah's finger guides them,
Through yonder purple arch ;
These Franks, sublimely silent,
Without a quickened breath,
Went, in the strength of duty,
Straight to their goal of death.

"If I were now to ask you
To name our bravest man,
Ye all at once would answer,
They called him Mehrab Khan.

He sleeps among his fathers,
Dear to our native land,
With the bright mark he bled for
Firm round his faithful hand.

"The songs they sing of Roostum
Fill all the past with light ;
If truth be in their music,
He was a noble knight.
But were these heroes living,
And strong for battle still,
Would Mehrab Khan, or Roostum,
Have climbed, like these, the Hill?"

And they replied : "Though Mehrab Khan was
    brave,
As chief, he chose himself what risks to run ;
Prince Roostum lied,[1] his forfeit life to save,
    Which these had never done."
    "Enough," he shouted fiercely,
    "Doomed though they be to Hell,
    Bind fast the crimson trophy
    Round BOTH wrists — bind it well.

---

[1] Roostum, overcome in the first instance, escaped death
by imposing upon the simple good faith of his son Sohrab,
whom he afterwards killed (ignorantly, of course).

" Who knows but that great Allah
May grudge such matchless men,
With none so decked in heaven,
To the fiends' flaming den? "

Then all those gallant robbers
Shouted a stern *Amen !*
They raised the slaughtered sergeant,
They raised his mangled ten.
And when we found their bodies,
Left bleaching in the wind,
Around *both* wrists in glory
That crimson thread was twined.

Then Napier's knightly heart, touched to the core,
Rang, like an echo, to that knightly deed ;
He bade its memory live for evermore,
    That those who run may read.

SIR FRANCIS HASTINGS DOYLE.

GEORGE NIDIVER.

Men have done brave deeds,
　　And bards have sung them well ;
I of good George Nidiver
　　Now the tale will tell.

In Californian mountains
　　A hunter bold was he ;
Keen his eye and sure his aim
　　As any you should see.

A little Indian boy
　　Followed him everywhere,
Eager to share the hunter's joy,
　　The hunter's meal to share.

And when the bird or deer
　　Fell by the hunter's skill,
The boy was always near
　　To help with right good-will.

14

One day as through the cleft
  Between two mountains steep,
Shut in both right and left,
  Their questing way they keep,

They see two grizzly bears,
  With hunger fierce and fell,
Rush at them unawares,
  Right down the narrow dell.

The boy turned round with screams,
  And ran with terror wild ;
One of the pair of savage beasts
  Pursued the shrieking child.

The hunter raised his gun, —
  He knew one charge was all, —
And through the boy's pursuing foe
  He sent his only ball.

The other on George Nidiver
  Came on with dreadful pace ;
The hunter stood unarmed,
  And met him face to face.

I say *unarmed* he stood :
  Against those frightful paws
The rifle-butt, or club of wood,
  Could stand no more than straws.

George Nidiver stood still,
   And looked him in the face ;
The wild beast stopped amazed,
   Then came with slackening pace.

Still firm the hunter stood,
   Although his heart beat high ;
Again the creature stopped,
   And gazed with wondering eye.

The hunter met his gaze,
   Nor yet an inch gave way ;
The bear turned slowly round,
   And slowly moved away.

What thoughts were in his mind
   It would be hard to spell ;
What thoughts were in George Nidiver
   I rather guess than tell.

But sure that rifle's aim,
   Swift choice of generous part,
Showed in its passing gleam
   The depths of a brave heart.

ANONYMOUS.

THE LOSS OF THE BIRKENHEAD:

SUPPOSED TO BE NARRATED BY A SOLDIER WHO SURVIVED.

FEBRUARY 25, 1852.

Every one must recollect how the soldiers on board the Birkenhead, lost off the coast of Africa by striking on a hidden rock,
sacrificed themselves, in order that the boats might be left free for
the women and children. These verses are put into the mouth of
one of the few who eventually escaped.

RIGHT on our flank the crimson sun went down,
  The deep sea rolled around in dark repose,
When, like the wild shriek from some captured
        town,
    A cry of women rose.

The stout ship Birkenhead lay hard and fast,
  Caught, without hope, upon a hidden rock;
Her timbers thrilled as nerves, when through them
        passed
    The spirit of that shock.

And ever like base cowards, who leave their ranks
    In danger's hour, before the rush of steel,
Drifted away, disorderly, the planks
        From underneath her keel.

Confusion spread, for, though the coast seemed
      near,
    Sharks hovered thick along that white sea-brink.
The boats could hold? — not all ; and it was clear
        She was about to sink.

"Out with those boats, and let us haste away,"
    Cried one, "ere yet yon sea the bark devours."
The man thus clamoring was, I scarce need say,
        No officer of ours.

We knew our duty better than to care
    For such loose babblers, and made no reply,
Till our good colonel gave the word, and there
        Formed us in line to die.

There rose no murmur from the ranks, no thought,
    By shameful strength, unhonored life to seek ;
Our post to quit we were not trained, nor taught
        To trample down the weak.

So we made women with their children go,
    The oars ply back again, and yet again ;
Whilst, inch by inch, the drowning ship sank low,
        Still under steadfast men.

What follows, why recall ?   The brave who died,
    Died without flinching in the bloody surf ;
They sleep as well, beneath that purple tide,
        As others, under turf ; —

They sleep as well, and, roused from their wild grave,
    Wearing their wounds like stars, shall rise again,
Joint-heirs with Christ, because they bled to save
        His weak ones, not in vain.

If that day's work no clasp or medal mark,
    If each proud heart no cross of bronze may press,
Nor cannon thunder loud from Tower and Park,
        This feel we, none the less :

That those whom God's high grace there saved
        from ill —
    Those also, left His martyrs in the bay —
Though not by siege, though not in battle, still
        Full well had earned their pay.

Sir Francis Hastings Doyle.

THE CHARGE OF THE LIGHT BRIGADE.

OCTOBER 25, 1854.

HALF a league, half a league,
　Half a league onward,
All in the valley of Death
　Rode the six hundred.
" Forward the Light Brigade !
Charge for the guns ! "　he said.
Into the valley of Death
　Rode the six hundred.

" Forward, the Light Brigade ! "
Was there a man dismayed?
Not though the soldier knew
　Some one had blundered ;
Theirs not to make reply,
Theirs not to reason why,
Theirs but to do and die,
Into the valley of Death
　Rode the six hundred.

Cannon to right of them,
Cannon to left of them,
Cannon in front of them
   Volleyed and thundered ;
Stormed at with shot and shell,
Boldly they rode and well,
Into the jaws of Death,
Into the mouth of Hell
   Rode the six hundred.

Flashed all their sabres bare,
Flashed as they turned in air,
Sabring the gunners there,
Charging an army, while
   All the world wondered.
Plunged in the battery-smoke
Right through the line they broke ;
Cossack and Russian
Reeled from the sabre-stroke
   Shattered and sundered.
Then they rode back, but not,
   Not the six hundred.

Cannon to right of them,
Cannon to left of them,
Cannon behind them
   Volleyed and thundered ;

Stormed at with shot and shell,
While horse and hero fell,
They that had fought so well
Came through the jaws of Death
Back from the mouth of Hell,
All that was left of them,
　　Left of six hundred.

When can their glory fade?
O the wild charge they made!
　　All the world wondered.
Honor the charge they made!
Honor the Light Brigade,
　　Noble six hundred!

ALFRED TENNYSON.

THE SONG OF THE CAMP.

"GIVE us a song!" the soldiers cried,
  The outer trenches guarding,
When the heated guns of the camps allied
  Grew weary of bombarding.

The dark Redan, in silent scoff,
  Lay, grim and threatening, under;
And the tawny mound of the Malakoff
  No longer belched its thunder.

There was a pause. A guardsman said:
  "We storm the forts to-morrow;
Sing while we may, another day
  Will bring enough of sorrow."

They lay along the battery's side,
  Below the smoking cannon, —
Brave hearts, from Severn and from Clyde,
  And from the banks of Shannon.

They sang of love, and not of fame;
  Forgot was Britain's glory;
Each heart recalled a different name,
  But all sang *Annie Laurie.*

Voice after voice caught up the song,
  Until its tender passion
Rose like an anthem, rich and strong,
  Their battle-eve confession.

Dear girl, her name he dared not speak,
  But, as the song grew louder,
Something upon the soldier's cheek
  Washed off the stains of powder.

Beyond the darkening ocean burned
  The bloody sunset's embers,
While the Crimean valleys learned
  How English love remembers.

And once again a fire of hell
  Rained on the Russian quarters,
With scream of shot, and burst of shell,
  And bellowing of the mortars !

And Irish Nora's eyes are dim
  For a singer, dumb and gory ;
And English Mary mourns for him
  Who sang of *Annie Laurie.*

Sleep, soldiers ! still in honored rest
    Your truth and valor wearing ;
The bravest are the tenderest, —
    The loving are the daring.

BAYARD TAYLOR.

THE RELIEF OF LUCKNOW.

SEPTEMBER 25, 1857.

OH, that last day in Lucknow fort !
  We knew that it was the last ;
That the enemy's mines had crept surely in,
  And the end was coming fast.

To yield to that foe meant worse than death ;
  And the men and we all worked on ;
It was one day more, of smoke and roar,
  And then it would all be done.

There was one of us, a corporal's wife,
  A fair, young, gentle thing,
Wasted with fever in the siege,
  And her mind was wandering.

She lay on the ground, in her Scottish plaid,
  And I took her head on my knee ;
"When my father comes hame frae the pleugh,"
      she said,
  " Oh ! then please wauken me ! "

She slept like a child on her father's floor,
　　In the flecking of woodbine shade,
When the house-dog sprawls by the open door,
　　And the mother's wheel is stayed.

It was smoke and roar and powder-stench,
　　And hopeless waiting for death ;
And the soldier's wife, like a full-tired child,
　　Seemed scarce to draw her breath.

I sank to sleep ; and I had my dream
　　Of an English village-lane,
And wall and garden ; — a sudden scream
　　Brought me back to the roar again.

There Jessie Brown stood listening ;
　　And then a broad gladness broke
All over her face, and she caught my hand
　　And drew me near and spoke :

" *The Highlanders !* oh, dinna ye hear?
　　The slogan far awa' ?
The McGregor's ? Ah ! I ken it weel ;
　　It 's the grandest o' them a' !

"God bless thae bonny Highlanders !
　　We 're saved ! we 're saved !" she cried ;
And fell on her knees, and thanks to God
　　Poured forth like a full flood-tide.

Along the battery-line her cry
    Had fallen among the men ;
And they started, for they were there to die ;
    Was life so near them, then?

They listened for life ; and the rattling fire
    Far off, and the far-off roar,
Were all ; and the colonel shook his head,
    And they turned to their guns once more.

But Jessie said : " That slogan's dune ;
    But can ye no hear them, noo,
The Campbells are comin ?   It's no a dream ;
    Our succors hae broken through ! "

We heard the roar and the rattle afar,
    But the pipes we could not hear ;
So the men plied their work of hopeless war,
    And knew that the end was near.

It was not long ere it must be heard,
    A shrilling, ceaseless sound ;
It was no noise of the strife afar,
    Or the sappers underground.

It *was* the pipes of the Highlanders !
    And now they played *Auld Lang Syne.*
It came to our men like the voice of God,
    And they shouted along the line.

And they wept and shook one another's hand,
  And the women sobbed in a crowd ;
And every one knelt down where we stood,
  And we all thanked God aloud.

That happy time when we welcomed them,
  Our men put Jessie first ;
And the general gave her his hand, and cheers
  From the men like a volley burst.

And the pipers' ribbons and tartan streamed,
  Marching round and round our line ;
And our joyful cheers were broken with tears,
  For the pipers played *Auld Lang Sync.*

ROBERT T. S. LOWELL.

Are there not many who remember (who can forget ?) that scene in the Sikh War, when the distant gleam of arms and flash of friendly uniform was descried by a little exhausted army among the hills, and the Scotch pipes struck up, *Oh ! but ye were lang a-comin !* The incident in the present case may not be historical, but it is true to nature, and intrinsically probable, which is all that poetry needs in that respect.

THE PRIVATE OF THE BUFFS.

"Some Sikhs, and a private of the Buffs, having remained behind with the grog-carts, fell into the hands of the Chinese. On
the next morning, they were brought before the authorities, and
commanded to perform the *kotou*. The Sikhs obeyed; but Moyse,
the English soldier, declaring that he would not prostrate himself
before any Chinaman alive, was immediately knocked upon the
head, and his body thrown on a dung-hill." — *China Correspondent
of the Times.*

Last night, among his fellow-roughs,
    He jested, quaffed, and swore ;
A drunken private of the Buffs,
    Who never looked before.
To-day, beneath the foeman's frown,
    He stands in Elgin's place,
Ambassador from Britain's crown,
    And type of all her race.

Poor, reckless, rude, low-born, untaught,
    Bewildered, and alone,
A heart with English instinct fraught
    He yet can call his own.

Aye, tear his body limb from limb,
  Bring cord, or axe, or flame ;
He only knows, that not through *him*
  Shall England come to shame.

Far Kentish [1] hop-fields round him seemed
  Like dreams to come and go ;
Bright leagues of cherry-blossoms gleamed,
  One sheet of living snow ;
The smoke above his father's door,
  In gray soft eddyings hung :
Must he then watch it rise no more,
  Doomed by himself so young?

Yes, honor calls ! With strength like steel
  He put the vision by ;
Let dusky Indians whine and kneel ;
  An English lad must die.
And thus, with eyes that would not shrink,
  With knee to man unbent,
Unfaltering on its dreadful brink,
  To his red grave he went.

Vain, mightiest fleets, of iron framed ;
  Vain, those all-shattering guns ;
Unless proud England keep, untamed,
  The strong heart of her sons.

[1] *The Buffs* are an East Kent Regiment.

So let his name through Europe ring —
    A man of mean estate,
Who died, as firm as Sparta's king,
    Because his soul was great.

Sir Francis Hastings Doyle.

SILVER-SHOE.

MOLTON STEEPLE RACES, — 1858.

THE sky was dimpled blue and white,
   The west was leaden gray,
Till in the east rose a fire of red,
   That burnt all the fog away.

The thorn-bush seemed new-dipped in blood,
   The firs were hung with cones,
The oaks were golden-green with moss,
   The birch wore its silver zones.

The deer with skins of a velvet pile
   Were feeding under the boughs
Of the oaks, that stretched their guarding arms
   Around the manor-house.

'T was *Oh !* for the glossy chestnut mare,
   And *Hurrah !* for the fiery roan,
But the caps went up like a cloud in the air
   For SILVER-SHOE alone.

We left the stable, where the door
　　Was nailed with winners' shoes,
And we trampled out to the crop-eared down
　　By laughing ones and twos.

The diamond seed of sprinkling dew
　　From the firs was shaking down,
As we cantered out by the dark-thorned trees,
　　And over the green hill-crown.

The chestnut mare was dancing mad,
　　The roan gave a snorting shout,
But you never heard a rolling cheer
　　Till SILVER-SHOE came out.

The starter waved his scarlet flag,
　　And then we stole along,
Past the line of rails and the nodding heads,
　　And past the thicker throng.

Gathering up, we trod, we trod,
　　Till like a boat well rowed,
Together went our hoofs thrown out,
　　So evenly we strode.

And now we skirt the crescent down,
　　Past the crimson-spotted thorns,
And away we go with a toss of hats
　　And a driving blast of horns.

Pad, pad together went our hoofs,
　　Ting, ting the rings and chains,
Chat, chat, chatter over the stones,
　　And splash through the red-clay lanes.

A white froth rose on our horses' mouths,
　　A lather on their hides,
And soon blood-drops from the rowel pricks
　　Oozed red from dripping sides.

There was a black mare, Yorkshire bred,
　　And the strong-built Irish gray,
But SILVER-SHOE was the only one
　　To show them all the way.

Strong and wide was his massy chest,
　　And bright his deep-brown eye ;
He could do anything but walk,
　　And everything but fly.

I knew the music of his feet
　　Over the hollow down ;
He was the chosen of the ten,
　　And the pet of Salisbury town.

Over we went, like skimming birds,
　　Clean over the wattled fence,
And crash through the bristling purple hedge,
　　With its thorny mailed defence.

The chestnut fell, at the water-leap,
  With its shining fourteen feet ;
At the double rail the roan broke down,
  But the black mare was not beat.

Together went our double shoes,
  Together went our stride,
Till I saw the blood in a crimson thread
  Run down Black Bessy's side.

I pushed him at the brook and hedge,
  And never touched a twig,
But I shuddered to see a stiff strong fence
  That rose up bold and big.

Now ghastly rose the rasping fence,
  Broad yawned the ditch below ;
I gave him head, and gave him spur,
  And let my wild blood go.

The black was down, and I was clear,
  Though staggering and blown ;
As I rode in trusty SILVER-SHOE
  His saddle seemed a throne.

The sky was spinning like a wheel,
  The trees were waltzing too,
As off I leaped, and clapped the flank
  Of the winner — SILVER-SHOE.

WALTER THORNBURY.

THE CUMBERLAND.

MARCH 8, 1862.

AT anchor in Hampton Roads we lay,
　　On board of the Cumberland, sloop-of-war ;
And at times from the fortress across the bay
　　　The alarum of drums swept past,
　　　Or a bugle blast
　　From the camp on the shore.

Then far away to the south uprose
　　A little feather of snow-white smoke,
And we knew that the iron ship of our foes
　　　Was steadily steering its course
　　　To try the force
　　Of our ribs of oak.

Down upon us heavily runs,
　　Silent and sullen, the floating fort ;
Then comes a puff of smoke from her guns,
　　　And leaps the terrible death,
　　　With fiery breath,
　　From each open port.

We are not idle, but send her straight
    Defiance back in a full broadside !
As hail rebounds from a roof of slate,
      Rebounds our heavier hail
      From each iron scale
    Of the monster's hide.

" Strike your flag ! " the Rebel cries,
    In his arrogant old plantation strain.
" Never ! " our gallant Morris replies ;
      " It is better to sink than to yield ! "
      And the whole air pealed
    With the cheers of our men.

Then, like a kraken huge and black,
    She crushed our ribs in her iron grasp !
Down went the Cumberland all a wreck,
      With a sudden shudder of death,
      And the cannon's breath
    For her dying gasp.

Next morn, as the sun rose over the bay,
    Still floated our flag at the mainmast-head.
Lord, how beautiful was thy day !
      Every waft of the air
      Was a whisper of prayer,
    Or a dirge for the dead.

Ho ! brave hearts that went down in the seas !
  Ye are at peace in the troubled stream ;
Ho ! brave land ! with hearts like these,
    Thy flag, that is rent in twain,
    Shall be one again,
  And without a seam !

HENRY WADSWORTH LONGFELLOW.

BARBARA FRIETCHIE.

SEPTEMBER 6, 1862.

UP from the meadows rich with corn,
Clear in the cool September morn,

The clustered spires of Frederick stand
Green-walled by the hills of Maryland.

Round about them orchards sweep,
Apple and peach tree fruited deep,

Fair as a garden of the Lord
To the eyes of the famished rebel horde,

On that pleasant morn of the early fall
When Lee marched over the mountain-wall, —

Over the mountains winding down,
Horse and foot, into Frederick town.

Forty flags with their silver stars,
Forty flags with their crimson bars,

Flapped in the morning wind ; the sun
Of noon looked down, and saw not one.

Up rose old Barbara Frietchie then,
Bowed with her fourscore years and ten ;

Bravest of all in Frederick town,
She took up the flag the men hauled down ;

In her attic window the staff she set,
To show that one heart was loyal yet.

Up the street came the rebel tread,
Stonewall Jackson riding ahead.

Under his slouched hat left and right
He glanced ; the old flag met his sight.

" Halt ! " — the dust-brown ranks stood fast ;
" Fire ! " — out blazed the rifle-blast.

It shivered the window, pane and sash ;
It rent the banner with seam and gash.

Quick, as it fell, from the broken staff
Dame Barbara seized the silken scarf ;

She leaned far out on the window-sill,
And shook it forth with a royal will.

" Shoot, if you must, this old, gray head,
But spare your country's flag," she said.

A shade of sadness, a blush of shame,
Over the face of the leader came ;

The nobler nature within him stirred
To life at that woman's deed and word :

" Who touches a hair of yon gray head
Dies like a dog ! March on !" he said.

All day long through Frederick street
Sounded the tread of marching feet :

All day long that free flag tost
Over the heads of the rebel host.

Ever its torn folds rose and fell
On the royal winds that loved it well ;

And through the hill-gaps sunset light
Shone over it with a warm good-night.

Barbara Frietchie's work is o'er,
And the Rebel rides on his raids no more.

Honor to her ! and let a tear
Fall, for her sake, on Stonewall's bier.

Over Barbara Frietchie's grave,
Flag of Freedom and Union, wave !

Peace, and order, and beauty draw
Round thy symbol of light and law ;

And ever the stars above look down
On thy stars below in Frederick town !

JOHN GREENLEAF WHITTIER.

THE OLD SERGEANT.[1]

THE carrier cannot sing to-night the ballads
    With which he used to go
Rhyming the grand round of the Happy New Years
    That are now beneath the snow ;

For the same awful and portentous shadow
    That overcast the earth,
And smote the land last year with desolation,
    Still darkens every hearth.

And the carrier hears Beethoven's mighty Dead-
      march
    Come up from every mart,
And he hears and feels it breathing in his bosom,
    And beating in his heart.

[1] This very remarkable poem was distributed, on the
first day of the year 1863, by the carriers of the Louisville
Journal.

And to-day, like a scarred and weather-beaten veteran,
　　Again he comes along,
To tell the story of the Old Year's struggles,
　　In another New Year's song.

And the song is his, but not so with the story ;
　　For the story, you must know,
Was told in prose to Assistant-Surgeon Austin,
　　By a soldier of Shiloh, —

By Robert Burton, who was brought up on the Adams,
　　With his death-wound in his side,
And who told the story to the Assistant-Surgeon
　　On the same night that he died.

But the singer feels it will better suit the ballad,
　　If all should deem it right,
To sing the story as if what it speaks of
　　Had happened but last night.

"Come a little nearer, doctor, — thank you, — let me
　　take the cup ;
Draw your chair up, — draw it closer, — just
　　another little sup !
Maybe you may think I 'm better ; but I 'm pretty
　　well used up, —
Doctor, you 've done all you could do, but I 'm
　　just a-going up !

" Feel my pulse, sir, if you want to, but it ain't
    much use to try — "
" Never say that," said the surgeon, as he smothered
    down a sigh ;
" It will never do, old comrade, for a soldier to say
    die ! "
" What you *say* will make no difference, doctor,
    when you come to die.

" Doctor, what has been the matter ? "   " You were
    very faint, they say ;
You must try to get some sleep now."   " Doctor,
    have I been away ? "
" Not that anybody knows of ! "   " Doctor, — doc-
    tor, please to stay !
There is something I must tell you, and you won't
    have long to stay !

" I have got my marching orders, and I 'm ready
    now to go ;
Doctor, did you say I fainted ? — but it could n't
    ha' been so, —
For as sure as I 'm a sergeant and was wounded at
    Shiloh,
I 've this very night been back there, on the old
    field of Shiloh !

" This is all that I remember ! The last time the
    lighter came,
And the lights had all been lowered, and the noises
    much the same,
He had not been gone five minutes before some-
    thing called my name :
ORDERLY SERGEANT — ROBERT BURTON ! just that
    way it called my name.

" And I wondered who could call me so distinctly
    and so slow,
Knew it could n't be the lighter, — he could not
    have spoken so, —
And I tried to answer, ' Here, sir ! ' but I could n't
    make it go !
For I could n't move a muscle, and I could n't make
    it go !

" Then I thought : ' It 's all a nightmare, all a hum-
    bug and a bore ;
Just another foolish *grapevine*,[1] — and it won't
    come any more ; '
But it came, sir, notwithstanding, just the same way
    as before :
ORDERLY SERGEANT — ROBERT BURTON ! even
    plainer than before.

[1] Army slang term for a *canard*, or false news.

" That is all that I remember, till a sudden burst of
    light,
And I stood beside the river, where we stood that
    Sunday night,
Waiting to be ferried over to the dark bluffs
    opposite,
When the river was perdition and all hell was
    opposite !

" And the same old palpitation came again in all its
    power,
And I heard a bugle sounding, as from some celes-
    tial tower ;
And the same mysterious voice said : ' IT IS THE
    ELEVENTH HOUR !
ORDERLY SERGEANT — ROBERT BURTON, — IT IS
    THE ELEVENTH HOUR ? '

" Doctor Austin ! what *day* is this ? "   " It is
    Wednesday night, you know."
"Yes, — to-morrow will be New Year's, and a right
    good time below !
What *time* is it, Doctor Austin ? "   " Nearly twelve."
        " Then don't you go !
Can it be that all this happened — all this — not
    an hour ago ?

" There was where the gunboats opened on the
      dark rebellious host ;
And where Webster semicircled his last guns upon
      the coast ;
There were still the two log-houses, just the same,
      or else their ghost, —
And the same old transport came and took me
      over, — or its ghost !

" And the old field lay before me all deserted far
      and wide ;
There was where they fell on Prentiss, — there
      McClernand met the tide ;
There was where stern Sherman rallied, and where
      Hurlbut's heroes died, —
Lower down where Wallace charged them, and kept
      charging till he died.

"There was where Lew Wallace showed them he
      was of the canny kin,
There was where old Nelson thundered, and where
      Rousseau waded in ;
There McCook sent 'em to breakfast, and we all
      began to win, —
There was where the grapeshot took me, just as we
      began to win.

"Now a shroud of snow and silence over everything
was spread;
And but for this old blue mantle and the old hat on
my head,
I should not have even doubted, to this moment, I
was dead, —
For my footsteps were as silent as the snow upon
the dead!

" Death and silence! death and silence! all around
me as I sped!
And behold a mighty tower, as if builded to the
dead,
To the heaven of the heavens, lifted up its mighty
head,
Till the stars and stripes of heaven all seemed
waving from its head!

" Round and mighty-based it towered, up into the
infinite, —
And I knew no mortal mason could have built a
shaft so bright;
For it shone like solid sunshine; and a winding
stair of light
Wound around it and around it, till it wound clear
out of sight!

"And behold as I approached it, with a rapt and
  dazzled stare, —
Thinking that I saw old comrades just ascending the
  great stair, —
Suddenly the solemn challenge broke of — 'Halt,
  and who goes there?'
'I'm a friend,' I said, 'if you are.' 'Then advance,
  sir, to the stair!'

"I advanced! — That sentry, doctor, was Elijah
  Ballantyne! —
First of all to fall on Monday, after we had formed
  the line! —
'Welcome, my old sergeant, welcome! Welcome
  by that countersign!'
And he pointed to the scar there, under this old
  cloak of mine!

"As he grasped my hand, I shuddered, thinking
  only of the grave;
But he smiled and pointed upward with a bright and
  bloodless glaive;
'That's the way, sir, to headquarters.' 'What
  headquarters?' 'Of the brave.'
'But the great tower?' 'That,' he answered, 'is
  the way, sir, of the brave!'

" Then a sudden shame came o'er me at his uniform
of light, —

At my own so old and tattered, and at his so new
and bright.

' Ah ! ' said he, ' you have forgotten the new uniform to-night, —

Hurry back, for you must be here at just twelve
o'clock to-night ! '

" And the next thing I remember, you were sitting
there, and I —

Doctor, — did you hear a footstep ? Hark ! — God
bless you all ! Good-by !

Doctor, please to give my musket and my knapsack,
when I die,

To my son — my son that 's coming, — he won't
get here till I die !

" Tell him his old father blessed him as he never did
before, —

And to carry that old musket " — Hark ! a knock
is at the door —

" Till the Union " — See ! it opens ! — " Father !
Father ! speak once more ! " —

" Bless you ! " gasped the old gray sergeant, and
he lay and said no more.

FORCEYTHE WILLSON.

"STONEWALL JACKSON'S WAY."

Come, stack arms, men! Pile on the rails,
   Stir up the camp-fire bright ;
No matter if the canteen fails,
   We 'll make a roaring night.
Here Shenandoah brawls along,
There burly Blue Ridge echoes strong,
To swell the brigade's rousing song
   Of " Stonewall Jackson's way."

We see him now — the old slouched hat
   Cocked o'er his eye askew,
The shrewd, dry smile, the speech so pat,
   So calm, so blunt, so true.
The " Blue-Light Elder " knows 'em well ;
Says he, " That 's Banks — he 's fond of shell,
Lord save his soul ! We 'll give him " — well,
   That 's " Stonewall Jackson's way."

Silence ! ground arms ! kneel all ! caps off !
    Old Blue-Light 's going to pray.
Strangle the fool that dares to scoff !
    Attention ! it 's his way.
Appealing from his native sod,
In *forma pauperis* to God —
" Lay bare thine arm, stretch forth thy rod !
    Amen ! " That 's " Stonewall's way."

He 's in the saddle now, — Fall in !
    Steady ! the whole brigade !
Hill's at the ford, cut off — we 'll win
    His way out, ball and blade !
What matter if our shoes are worn ?
What matter if our feet are torn ?
" Quick-step ! we 're with him before dawn ! "
    That 's " Stonewall Jackson's way."

The sun's bright lances rout the mists
    Of morning, and, by George !
Here 's Longstreet struggling in the lists,
    Hemmed in an ugly gorge.
Pope and his Yankees, whipped before, —
" Bay'nets and grape ! " hear Stonewall roar ;
" Charge, Stuart ! Pay off Ashby's score ! "
    In " Stonewall Jackson's way."

Ah ! maiden, wait and watch and yearn
   For news of Stonewall's band !
Ah ! widow, read with eyes that burn
   That ring upon thy hand.
Ah ! wife, sew on, pray on, hope on !
Thy life shall not be all forlorn ;
The foe had better ne'er been born
   That gets in " Stonewall's way."

ANONYMOUS.

CAVALRY SONG.

From " Alice of Monmouth."

OUR good steeds snuff the evening air,
   Our pulses with their purpose tingle ;
The foeman's fires are twinkling there ;
   He leaps to hear our sabres jingle !
        HALT !
Each carbine send its whizzing ball !
Now, cling ! clang ! forward all,
       Into the fight !

Dash on beneath the smoking dome.
   Through level lightnings gallop nearer !
One look to Heaven !   No thoughts of home :
   The guidons that we bear are dearer.
        CHARGE !
Cling ! Clang ! forward all !
Heaven help those whose horses fall !
       Cut left and right !

They flee before our fierce attack !
　They fall ! they spread in broken surges !
Now, comrades, bear our wounded back,
　And leave the foeman to his dirges.
　　　　Wheel !
The bugle sounds the swift recall :
Cling ! Clang ! forward all !
　　　Home, and good-night !

Edmund C. Stedman.

THE COLOR-BEARER.

VICKSBURG, MAY 22, 1863.

" The storming party looked in vain for the support which had been promised it. The brigade which had been ordered to follow it hesitated. Finally, all but one of the one hundred and fifty got discouraged, and sought the shelter of a deep ravine. William Trogden, a private of Company B, Eighth Missouri, refused to re-trace a single step. He was color-bearer of the storming party. When his comrades left him, he dug a hole in the ground with his bayonet, planted his flag-staff in it, within twenty yards of the enemy's rifle-pits, and sat down by the side of his banner, where he remained all day." — *Report of the Assault on Vicksburg.*

LET them go ! — they are brave, I know —
   But a berth like this, why it suits me best ;
   I can't carry back the Old Colors to-day,
We 've come together a long rough way —
   Here 's as good a spot as any to rest.

No look, I reckon, to hold them long ;
   So here, in the turf, with my bayonet,
To dig for a bit, and plant them strong —
   (Look out for the point — we may want it yet !)

Dry work ! but the old canteen holds fast
    A few drops of water — not over-fresh —
So, for a drink ! — it may be the last —
    My respects to you, Mr. Secesh !

No great show for the snakes to sight :
    Our boys keep 'em busy yet, by the powers ! —
Hark, what a row going on, to the Right !
    Better luck there, I hope, than ours.

Half an hour ! — (and you 'd swear 't was three) —
    Here by the bully old staff, I 've sat —
Long enough, as it seems to me,
    To lose as many lives as a cat.

Now and then, they sputter away ;
    A puff and a crack, and I hear the ball.
Mighty poor shooting, I should say —
    Not bad fellows, may be, after all.

My chance, of course, is n't worth a dime —
    But I thought, 't would be over, sudden and quick ;
Well, since it seems that we 're not on time,
    Here 's for a touch of the Kilikinick.

Cool as a clock ! — and, what is strange —
    Out of this dream of death and alarm,
(This wild hard week of battle and change) —
Out of the rifle's deadly range —
    My thoughts are all at the dear old farm.

'T is green as a sward, by this, I know —
   The orchard is just beginning to set,
They mowed the home-lot a week ago —
   The corn must be late, for that piece is wet.

I can think of one or two, that would wipe
   A drop or so from a soft blue eye,
To see me sit, and puff at my pipe,
   With a hundred death's heads grinning hard by.

And I wonder, when this has all passed o'er,
   And the tattered old stars in triumph wave on
Through street and square, with welcoming roar,
   If ever they 'll think of us who are gone?

How we marched together, sound or sick,
   Sank in the trench o'er the heavy spade —
How we charged on the guns, at double-quick —
Kept rank for Death to choose and pick —
   And lay on the bed no fair hands made.

Ah, well ! at last, when the Nation 's free,
   And flags are flapping from bluff to bay,
In old St. Lou, what a time there 'll be !
I may n't be there, the Hurrah to see —
   But if the Old Rag goes back to-day,
   They never shall say 't was carried by me !

HENRY HOWARD BROWNELL.

SHERIDAN'S RIDE.

OCTOBER 19, 1864.

Up from the South at break of day,
Bringing to Winchester fresh dismay,
The affrighted air with a shudder bore,
Like a herald in haste, to the chieftain's door,
The terrible grumble, and rumble, and roar,
Telling the battle was on once more,
And Sheridan twenty miles away.

And wider still those billows of war
Thundered along the horizon's bar ;
And louder yet into Winchester rolled
The roar of that red sea uncontrolled,
Making the blood of the listener cold,
As he thought of the stake in that fiery fray,
And Sheridan twenty miles away.

But there is a road from Winchester town,
A good broad highway leading down ;
And there, through the flush of the morning light,

A steed as black as the steeds of night,
Was seen to pass, as with eagle flight,
As if he knew the terrible need ;
He stretched away with his utmost speed ;
Hills rose and fell ; but his heart was gay,
With Sheridan fifteen miles away.

Still sprung from those swift hoofs, thundering South,
The dust, like smoke from the cannon's mouth ;
Or a trail of a comet, sweeping faster and faster,
Foreboding to traitors the doom of disaster.
The heart of the steed and the heart of the master
Were beating like prisoners assaulting their walls,
Impatient to be where the battle-field calls ;
Every nerve of the charger was strained to full play,
With Sheridan only ten miles away.

Under his spurning feet the road
Like an arrowy Alpine river flowed,
And the landscape sped away behind
Like an ocean flying before the wind ;
And the steed, like a bark fed with furnace ire,
Swept on with his wild eye full of fire.
But lo ! he is nearing his heart's desire ;
He is snuffing the smoke of the roaring fray,
With Sheridan only five miles away.

17

The first that the General saw were the groups
Of stragglers, and then the retreating troops.
What was done? what to do? A glance told him
　　both.
Then, striking his spurs, with a terrible oath,
He dashed down the line, mid a storm of huzzas,
And the wave of retreat checked its course there,
　　because
The sight of the master compelled it to pause.
With foam and with dust the black charger was gray ;
By the flash of his eye, and the red nostril's play,
He seemed to the whole great army to say,
" I have brought you Sheridan all the way
From Winchester down to save the day ! "

Hurrah ! hurrah for Sheridan !
Hurrah ! hurrah for horse and man !
And when their statues are placed on high,
Under the dome of the Union sky,
The American soldier's Temple of Fame, —
There with the glorious General's name,
Be it said, in letters both bold and bright,
" Here is the steed that saved the day
By carrying Sheridan into the fight,
From Winchester, twenty miles away ! "

THOMAS BUCHANAN READ.

BIVOUAC OF THE DEAD.

THE muffled drum's sad roll has beat
    The soldier's last tattoo ;
No more on Life's parade shall meet
    That brave and fallen few.
On Fame's eternal camping-ground
    Their silent tents are spread,
And Glory guards, with solemn round,
    The bivouac of the dead.

THEODORE O'HARA.

ODE.

How sleep the brave, who sink to rest
By all their country's wishes blessed !
When Spring, with dewy fingers cold,
Returns to deck their hallowed mould,
She there shall dress a sweeter sod
Than Fancy's feet have ever trod.

By fairy hands their knell is rung ;
By forms unseen their dirge is sung ;
There Honor comes, a pilgrim gray,
To bless the turf that wraps their clay ;
And Freedom shall awhile repair,
To dwell a weeping hermit there !

WILLIAM COLLINS.

ODE RECITED AT THE HARVARD COMMEMORATION.

JULY 21, 1865.

. . . .

MANY loved Truth, and lavished life's best oil
    Amid the dust of books to find her,
Content at last, for guerdon of their toil,
    With the cast mantle she hath left behind her.
      Many in sad faith sought for her,
      Many with crossed hands sighed for her;
      But these, our brothers, fought for her,
      At life's dear peril wrought for her,
      So loved her that they died for her,
      Tasting the raptured fleetness
      Of her divine completeness :
        Their higher instinct knew
Those love her best who to themselves are true,
And what they dare to dream of dare to do ;
      They followed her and found her
      Where all may hope to find,
Not in the ashes of the burnt-out mind,
But beautiful, with danger's sweetness round her ;

Where faith made whole with deed
Breathes its awakening breath
Into the lifeless creed,
They saw her plumed and mailed,
With sweet, stern face unveiled,
And all-repaying eyes, look proud on them in death.

.   .   .   .   .   .

Life may be given in many ways,
  And loyalty to Truth be sealed
As bravely in the closet as the field,
    So generous is Fate ;
    But then to stand beside her
    When craven churls deride her,
To front a lie in arms and not to yield, —
    This shows, methinks, God's plan
    And measure of a stalwart man,
    Limbed like the old heroic breeds,
    Who stand self-poised on manhood's solid
      earth,
    Not forced to frame excuses for his birth,
Fed from within with all the strength he needs.

.   .   .   .   .   .

We sit here in the Promised Land
That flows with Freedom's honey and milk ;
But 't was they won it, sword in hand,
Making the nettle danger soft for us as silk.

We welcome back our bravest and our best ; —
Ah, me ! not all ! some come not with the rest,
Who went forth brave and bright as any here !
I strive to mix some gladness with my strain,
  But the sad strings complain,
  And will not please the ear ;
I sweep them for a pæan, but they wane
   Again and yet again
Into a dirge, and die away in pain.
In these brave ranks I only see the gaps,
Thinking of dear ones whom the dumb turf wraps,
Dark to the triumph which they died to gain :
  Fitlier may others greet the living,
  For me the past is unforgiving ;
   I with uncovered head
   Salute the sacred dead,
Who went, and who return not. — Say not so !
'T is not the grapes of Canaan that repay,
But the high faith that failed not by the way ;
Virtue treads paths that end not in the grave ;
No ban of endless night exiles the brave ;
   And to the saner mind
We rather seem the dead that stayed behind.
Blow, trumpets, all your exultations blow !
For never shall their aureoled presence lack :
I see them muster in a gleaming row,
With ever-youthful brows that nobler show ;
We find in our dull road their shining track ;

In every nobler mood
We feel the orient of their spirit glow,
Part of our life's unalterable good,
Of all our saintlier aspiration ;
        They come transfigured back,
Secure from change in their high-hearted ways,
Beautiful evermore, and with the rays
Of morn on their white Shields of Expectation !
            .   .   .   .

Bow down, dear Land, for thou hast found release !
    Thy God, in these distempered days,
    Hath taught thee the sure wisdom of His ways,
And through thine enemies hath wrought thy peace !
        Bow down in prayer and praise !
O Beautiful ! my Country ! ours once more !
Smoothing thy gold of war-dishevelled hair
O'er such sweet brows as never other wore,
        And letting thy set lips,
        Freed from wrath's pale eclipse,
    The rosy edges of their smile lay bare,
What words divine of lover or of poet
Could tell our love and make thee know it,
    Among the Nations bright beyond compare ?
        What were our lives without thee ?
        What all our lives to save thee ?
        We reck not what we gave thee ;
        We will not dare to doubt thee,
    But ask whatever else, and we will dare !

                    JAMES RUSSELL LOWELL.

HISTORICAL NOTES.

HISTORICAL NOTES.

Horatius, page 1.

"THIS ballad is supposed to have been made about a hundred and twenty years after the war which it celebrates, and just before the taking of Rome by the Gauls. The author seems to have been an honest citizen, proud of the military glory of his country, sick of the disputes of factions, and much given to pining after good old times which had never really existed. The allusion, however, to the partial manner in which the public lands were allotted could proceed only from a plebeian; and the allusion to the fraudulent sale of spoils marks the date of the poem, and shows that the poet shared in the general discontent with which the proceedings of Camillus, after the taking of Veii, were regarded." — MACAULAY.

Alfred the Harper, page 27.

"A popular legend relates that Alfred, early in 878, not daring to rely on any evidence but that of his own senses as to the numbers, disposition, and discipline of the Danish army, assumed the garb of a minstrel, and, with one attendant, visited the camp of Guthrum. Here he stayed, 'showing tricks and making sport,' until he had penetrated to the King's tents, and learned all that he wished to know. After satisfying himself as to the chances of a sudden attack, he returned to Athelney, and not long after gained the decisive victory of Ethandune, which established his rule." — THOMAS HUGHES.

Garci Perez de Vargas, page 37.

" The crowns of Castile and Leon being at length joined
in the person of King Ferdinand, surnamed El Santo, the
authority of the Moors in Spain was destined to receive
many severe blows from the united efforts of two Christian
states, which had in former times too often exerted their
vigor against each other. The most important event of
King Ferdinand's reign was the conquest of Seville, which
great city yielded to his arms in the year 1248, after sustain-
ing a long and arduous siege of sixteen months. Don
Garci Perez de Vargas was one of the most distinguished
warriors who then fought under the banners of Ferdinand.

Sir Patrick Spens, page 42.

The event upon which this ballad is founded has been
the subject of considerable discussion. Some maintain that
it refers to the marriage of James III. with the Princess of
Norway and Denmark; others believe it to refer to the expedition sent in 1290 to bring home Margaret, the Maid of
Norway, after the death of her father, Alexander III. The
weight of testimony is in favor of its bearing reference to
the fate of the expedition which, in 1281, carried the same
Margaret to Norway, as the bride of King Eric. Mr.
Robert Chambers translates from Fordoun the following
account of the incident : " A little before this, namely, in
the year 1281, Margaret, daughter of Alexander III., was
married to the King of Norway; who, leaving Scotland on
the last day of July, was conveyed thither, in noble style, in
company with many knights and nobles. In returning
home, after the celebration of her nuptials, the Abbot of
Balmerinoch, Bernard of Monte-Alto, and many other
persons were drowned."

Bannockburn, page 47.

The great battle of Bannockburn was fought on June
24, 1314. Robert Bruce, with 30,000 or 40,000 Scotch,

gained a signal victory over Edward II., with 100,000 English, and secured his throne and the independence of Scotland. The English are said to have lost 30,000 men, and the Scotch 8,000 men.

Battle of Otterbourne, page 52.

"James, Earl of Douglas, with his brother the Earl of Murray, in 1388 invaded Northumberland, at the head of 3,000 men; while the Earls of Fife and Strathern, sons to the king of Scotland, ravaged the western borders of England, with a still more numerous army. Douglas penetrated as far as Newcastle, where the renowned Hotspur lay in garrison. In a skirmish before the walls, Percy's lance, with the pennon, or guidon, attached to it, was taken by Douglas, as most authors affirm, in a personal encounter betwixt the two heroes. The earl shook the pennon aloft, and swore he would carry it as his spoil into Scotland, and plant it upon his castle of Dalkeith. 'That,' answered Percy, 'shalt thou never!' Accordingly, having collected the forces of the Marches, to a number equal, or (according to the Scottish historians) much superior, to the army of Douglas, Hotspur made a night attack upon the Scottish camp, at Otterbourne, about thirty-two miles from Newcastle. An action took place, fought by moonlight, with uncommon gallantry and desperation. At length, Douglas, armed with an iron mace, which few but he could wield, rushed into the thickest of the English battalions, followed only by his chaplain, and two squires of his body. Before his followers could come up, their brave leader was stretched on the ground, with three mortal wounds; his squires lay dead by his side; the priest alone, armed with a lance, was protecting his master from farther injury. 'I die like my forefathers,' said the expiring hero, 'in a field of battle, and not on a bed of sickness. Conceal my death; defend my standards, and avenge my fall! it is an old prophecy that a dead man shall gain a field, and I hope it will be accomplished this night.' . . .

When morning appeared, victory began to incline to the Scottish side. Ralph Percy, brother to Hotspur, was made prisoner, and, shortly after, Harry Percy himself was taken by Lord Montgomery. The number of the captives nearly equalled that of the victors. Upon this the English retired, and left the Scots masters of the dear-bought honors of the field. The field was fought August 15, 1388."— SIR WALTER SCOTT.

Chevy-Chace, page 59.

"With regard to the subject of this ballad, although it has no countenance from history, there is room to think it had originally some foundation in fact. It was one of the laws of the Marches, frequently renewed between the nations, that neither party should hunt in the other's borders, without leave from the proprietors or their deputies. There had long been a rivalship between the two martial families of Percy and Douglas, which, heightened by the national quarrel, must have produced frequent challenges and struggles for superiority, petty invasions of their respective domains, and sharp contests for the point of honor, which would not always be recorded in history. Something of this kind, we may suppose, gave rise to the ancient ballad of the *Hunting the Cheviot* [the original form of *Chevy-Chace*]. Percy, Earl of Northumberland, had vowed to hunt for three days in the Scottish border, without condescending to ask leave from Earl Douglas, who was either lord of the soil, or lord-warden of the Marches. Douglas would not fail to resent the insult, and endeavor to repel the intruders by force. This would naturally produce a sharp conflict between the two parties; something of which, it is probable, did really happen, though not attended with the tragical circumstances recorded in the ballad; for these are evidently borrowed from the Battle of Otterbourne, a very different event, but which after-times would easily confound with it."
— PERCY.

The ballad may refer to the battle of Pepperden, fought in 1436, between the son of Hotspur and Earl William Douglas, of Angus, with a small army of four thousand men each, in which the latter had the advantage.

Battle of Harlaw, page 71.

This battle took place at Harlaw, near Aberdeen, on the 24th of July, 1411. The conflict was occasioned by a dispute concerning the succession to the earldom of Ross, between Donald, Lord of the Isles, and the son of the Regent, Robert, Duke of Albany, whose claim was supported by Alexander Stuart, Earl of Mar. The consequences of this battle were of the highest importance, inasmuch as the wild Celts of the Highlands and Islands received such a check that they never again combined for the conquest of the civilized parts of Scotland.

Pibroch of Donuil Dhu, page 77.

"This is a very ancient pibroch belonging to Clan MacDonald, and supposed to refer to the expedition of Donald Balloch, who, in 1431, launched from the Isles with a considerable force, invaded Lochaber, and at Inverlochy defeated and put to flight the Earls of Mar and Caithness, though at the head of an army superior to his own." — SIR WALTER SCOTT.

Edinburgh after Flodden, page 83.

"The great and disastrous battle of Flodden was fought upon the 9th of September, 1513. The Scottish army was totally defeated, with a loss of ten thousand men. Of these, a great proportion were of high rank; the remainder being composed of the gentry, the farmers, and landed yeomanry, who disdained to fly when their sovereign and his nobles lay stretched in heaps around them. Besides their King, James IV., the Archbishop of St. Andrew's, thirteen earls, two bishops, two abbots, and fifteen lords and chiefs of clans perished.

"The loss to Edinburgh was peculiarly great. All the magistrates and able-bodied citizens had followed their king to Flodden, whence very few of them returned. The consternation in the city was excessive. But the English had themselves suffered losses so severe that Surrey was not able to follow up his victory, and soon after was compelled to disband his army."

The city banner, referred to in the poem, was presented to the burghers of Edinburgh by James III., in return for their loyal service of 1482. It is still in existence, and held in honor and reverence.

The Revenge, page 109.

Sir Richard Grenville, in a single bark, the Revenge, found himself girt in by fifty men-of-war, each twice as large as his own. He held out from afternoon to the following daybreak, beating off attempt after attempt to board him; and it was not till his powder was spent, more than half his crew killed and the rest wounded, that the ship struck its flag. Grenville had refused to surrender, and was carried, mortally wounded, to die in a Spanish ship. "Here die I, Richard Grenville," were his last words, "with a joyful and quiet mind, for that I have ended my life as a good soldier ought to do, who has fought for his country and his queen, for honor and religion." August, 1591. — *History of the English People*, by John Richard Green, vol. ii., p. 451, Harper's edition.

See also J. A. Froude's essay on "England's Forgotten Worthies," in *Short Studies on Great Subjects*, 1st series.

Kinmont Willie, page 117.

In 1596, at a time of truce, when he should have been safe, William Armstrong of Kinmonth, a Scottish borderer, was waylaid by a large company of English, and taken as a prisoner to Carlisle Castle, there to be soon executed.

Lord Buccleugh, not being able to get redress, resolved to set him free, and succeeded in so doing, in the manner related in the ballad. Queen Elizabeth was much incensed at having one of her chief castles surprised, and a prisoner taken from the hands of the warder and carried away, but no serious results followed. Buccleugh was sent to England as a hostage, and, according to ancient family traditions, was presented to the Queen, who demanded of him how he "dared to undertake an enterprise so desperate and presumptuous." "What is it," he replied, "that a man dares not do?" Struck with the reply, Elizabeth turned to a lord-in-waiting, and said: "With ten thousand such men our brother of Scotland might shake the firmest throne of Europe."

The Execution of Montrose, page 135.

"There is no ingredient of fiction in the historical incidents recorded in the following ballad. The indignities that were heaped upon Montrose during his procession through Edinburgh, his appearance before the Estates, and his last passage to the scaffold, as well as his undaunted bearing, have all been spoken of by eye-witnesses of the scene."

The "great Marquis" was born in 1612. Between 1637 and 1640 he sided with the Covenanting party, but in 1640, when an open rupture took place between the King and the Covenanters, he took a different position, and, in 1644, openly espoused the cause of the King, and became an invaluable assistance to him. He gained many victories, and displayed great bravery; but was surprised and defeated at Philiphaugh, September 13, 1645, and Charles induced him to leave the kingdom. He was in Holland when he received the news of the execution of Charles, and he attempted a fresh invasion of Scotland, in behalf of the exiled son of that monarch. But he was entirely unsuccessful, and was delivered up to his enemies. Condemned to death as a traitor to the Covenant, he was executed May 21, 1650. 18

"The ballad may be considered as a narrative related by an aged Highlander, who had followed Montrose throughout his campaigns, to his grandson, shortly before the battle of Killiecrankie."

Barclay of Ury, page 147.

"Among the earliest converts to the doctrines of Friends, in Scotland, was Barclay of Ury, an old and distinguished soldier, who had fought under Gustavus Adolphus, in Germany. As a Quaker, he became the object of persecution and abuse at the hands of the magistrates and the populace. None bore the indignities of the mob with greater patience and nobleness of soul than this once proud gentleman and soldier. One of his friends, on an occasion of uncommon rudeness, lamented that he should be treated so harshly in his old age, who had been so honored before. 'I find more satisfaction,' said Barclay, 'as well as honor, in being thus insulted for my religious principles, than when, a few years ago, it was usual for the magistrates, as I passed the city of Aberdeen, to meet me on the road and conduct me to public entertainment in their hall, and then escort me out again, to gain my favor.' " — J. G. WHITTIER.

The Burial-March of Dundee, page 156.

John Graham of Claverhouse, Viscount Dundee, was born in 1643. He served in the French and Dutch service, and in 1678 returned to Scotland, where he engaged in the work of suppressing the Covenanters. He was defeated at Drumclog in 1679; but a few weeks after, gained the victory of Bothwell Bridge. Ten years later he raised the standard of rebellion against the government of William and Mary, being loyal to his fallen master, James II., and was killed at the Pass of Killiecrankie, July 27, 1689, in the hour of victory. Sir Walter Scott says of him, in a note to *Old Mortality* : "This remarkable person united the seemingly inconsistent qualities of courage and cruelty, a disinterested and devoted loyalty to his prince, with a disregard of the rights of his fellow-subjects. He was the unscrupulous agent of the Scottish Privy Council, in executing the merciless severities of the Government in Scotland during the reigns of Charles II. and James II.; but he redeemed his character by the zeal with which he asserted the cause of the latter monarch after the Revolution, the military skill with which he supported it at the battle of Killiecrankie, and by his own death in the arms of victory."

The Island of the Scots, page 166.

In consequence of a capitulation with Government, the regular troops who had served under Lord Dundee were conveyed to France. (Dundee had fallen in the battle of the Pass of Killiecrankie, in 1689.) After a time, the officers, being unwilling to depend indefinitely on the bounty of the French King, formed themselves into a company of private soldiers, numbering about a hundred and twenty, and served for several campaigns with the French army. They met with losses and were reduced to need, but maintained a heroic spirit. Their last exploit was in December, 1697. The Germans had carried a bridge over to an island in the middle of the Rhine, and intrenched themselves there with five hundred men; and their guns were extremely galling to the French camp. The French were waiting for boats, as the water was very deep, when the Scotch company proposed to wade the river and attack the Germans. They secured their arms round their necks, waded into the river hand in hand, and, having crossed, fell upon the Germans, and drove them from the island. They kept possession of it for nearly six weeks, until the Germans drew off their army and retreated.

Song of Marion's Men, page 183.

Francis Marion was a colonel in the Continental Army. He was made a brigadier-general by Governor Rutledge of South Carolina, and distinguished himself by conducting a

vigorous partisan, or guerilla, warfare against the British in
the latter part of the Revolutionary War. "The British
troops were so harassed by the irregular and successful warfare which he kept up at the head of a few daring followers,
that they sent an officer to remonstrate with him for not
coming into the open field, and fighting like a gentleman
and a Christian." Irving gives the following description of
him : —

"He was nearly fifty years of age, and small of stature,
but hardy, healthy, and vigorous; brave, but not braggart,
never avoiding danger, but never rashly seeking it; taci-
turn and abstemious; a strict disciplinarian; careful of the
lives of his men, but little mindful of his own life; just in
his dealings, free from everything selfish or mercenary, and
incapable of a meanness. He had his haunts and strong-
holds in the morasses of the Pedee and Black Rivers. His
men were hardy and abstemious as himself; they ate their
meat without salt, often subsisted on potatoes, were scantily
clad, and almost destitute of blankets. Marion was full of
stratagems and expedients. Sallying forth from his morasses, he would overrun the lower districts, pass the Santee,
beat up the small posts in the vicinity of Charleston, cut up
the communication between that city and Camden; and,
having struck some signal blow, so as to rouse the vengeance
of the enemy, would retreat again into his fenny fastnesses.
Hence the British gave him the by-name of the *Swamp
Fox;* but those of his countrymen who knew his courage,
his loftiness of spirit, and spotless integrity, considered him
the *Bayard of the South.*"

The Burial of Sir John Moore, page 194.

After the capture of Madrid by Napoleon, Sir John
Moore conducted a masterly retreat, under great difficul-
ties, from Astorga to the coast, nearly 250 miles. On
reaching Corunna, he was compelled to fight with the
forces of Soult and Ney, in order to cover the embarkation

of his troops. The English were victorious, though of inferior numbers; but their gallant general fell. He was buried on the ramparts in his military cloak.

Marco Bozzaris, page 196.

Marco Bozzaris was a Greek patriot who distinguished himself in the early part of the modern War of Independence. He was born at Suli, in the mountains of the Epirus, towards the close of the eighteenth century. On the 20th of August, 1823, he advanced swiftly at the head of 1,200 men, and at night burst in upon the Turkish camp of 4,000 men at Laspi, the site of the ancient Platæa. The Turks were routed with great slaughter; and the victors captured their camp, standards, and a vast quantity of baggage. This triumph was saddened by the loss of the heroic Bozzaris, who fell while leading his men on to the final attack. His last words were: " To die for liberty is a pleasure, and not a pain."

Old Ironsides, page 201.

The frigate Constitution was known as Old Ironsides, because of her victories over the English in the War of 1812. This poem was called forth by a proposal, in 1830, to break her up, and sell the iron and timber.

The Red Thread of Honor, page 203.

" A sergeant and ten men of the Thirteenth got on the wrong side of a small ravine, and came to the foot of a rocky platform crowned by the enemy, and where the ravine suddenly deepened to a frightful chasm. The sergeant saw his officer, and the main body beyond, gesticulating because they saw the enemy above. They were beckoning to retreat; he thought it was to go on, and at once the stern veterans climbed the rocks. As they leaped on to the platform, the enemy, eighty in number, fell on them, sword in hand, and the fight was desperate.

Seventeen hill-men were slain, six of the soldiers; and the rest, wounded and overborne, were dashed over the edge, and rolled down. Amongst the tribes, when a warrior dies with noted bravery, a red or green string is tied round the wrist of the corpse, the red being of most honor ; here, before casting the bodies of the slain down from the platform, they tied a red string on both wrists." — Sir Charles Napier.

The Loss of the Birkenhead, page 212.

Captain Wright, of the Ninety-first, writes : " The order and regularity that prevailed on board, from the time the ship struck till she totally disappeared, far exceeded anything that I thought could be effected by the best discipline. Every one did as he was directed, and there was not a murmur nor a cry among them till the vessel made her final plunge."

Of 630 officers, seamen, soldiers, and boys on board, 438 were drowned.

The Charge of the Light Brigade, page 215.

The Crimean War was waged by England and France against Russia, in defence of the Turkish Empire. " The war gathered round the fortress of Sebastopol on the Black Sea, which was besieged by the allies ; but the besiegers were soon besieged in their turn by the increasing masses of Russian troops, who not only attacked the positions they held on the plateau south of the town, but strove to cut them off from Balaklava, their main harbor.

" The Russians attacked the allies fiercely on Oct. 25, 1854, in the hope of obtaining possession of Balaklava. The attempt was bold and brilliant, but it was splendidly repulsed. The cavalry particularly distinguished themselves. It will be memorable in all English history as the battle in which occurred the famous Charge of the Light Brigade. Owing to some fatal misconception of the meaning of an order from the commander-in-chief, the Light Brigade, 607 men in all, charged what has been rightly described as 'the Russian army in position.'" Of the 607 men 198 came back.

The Cumberland, page 232.

LIEUTENANT MORRIS'S REPORT.

NEWPORT NEWS, VA., March 9, 1862.

SIR, — Yesterday morning, at nine A.M., I discovered two steamers at anchor off Smithfield Point, on the left-hand, or western, side of the river, distant about twelve miles. At twelve meridian I discovered three vessels under steam, standing down the Elizabeth River, toward Sewall's Point. I beat to quarters, double-breeched the guns on the main deck, and cleared ship for action.

At one P.M. the enemy hove in sight, gradually nearing us. The ironclad steamer Merrimac, accompanied by two steam-gunboats, passed ahead of the Congress frigate, and steered down toward us. We opened fire on her. She stood on, and struck us under the starboard fore-channels. She delivered her fire at the same time. The destruction was great. We returned the fire with solid shot, with alacrity.

At thirty minutes past three the water had gained upon us, notwithstanding the pumps were kept actively employed, to a degree that, the forward magazine being drowned, we had to take powder from the after magazine for the ten-inch gun. At thirty-five minutes past three the water had risen to the main hatchway, and the ship canted to port; and we delivered a parting fire, each man trying to save himself by jumping overboard.

Timely notice was given, and all the wounded who could walk were ordered out of the cock-pit; but those of the wounded who had been carried into the sick-bay and on the berth-deck were so mangled that it was impossible to save them.

It is impossible for me to individualize. Alike, the officers and men all behaved in the most gallant manner. Lieutenant Selfridge and Master Stuyvesant were in command of the gun-deck divisions, and they did all that noble and gallant officers could do. Acting-Masters Randall and Kennison, who had charge each of a pivot-gun, showed the most perfect coolness, and did all they could to save our noble ship; but, I am sorry to say, without avail. Among the last to leave the ship were Sergeant Martin and Assistant-Surgeon Kershaw, who did all they could for the wounded, promptly and faithfully.

The loss we sustained I cannot yet inform you of, but it has been very great. The warrant and steerage officers could not have been more prompt and active than they were at their different stations. Chaplain Lenhart is missing. Master's-mate John Harrington was killed. I should judge we have lost upward of one hundred men. I can only say, in conclusion, that all did their duty, and we sank with the American flag flying at the peak.

I am, sir, &c.,

GEORGE M. MORRIS,
Lieutenant and Executive Officer.

Sheridan's Ride, page 256.

CEDAR CREEK, VA., Oct. 19, 10 P.M.

LIEUTENANT-GENERAL GRANT, *City Point*, —

I have the honor to report that my army at Cedar Creek was attacked at Alacken this morning, before daylight, and my left was turned and driven in, in confusion. In fact, most of the line was driven in confusion, with the loss of twenty pieces of artillery. I hastened from Winchester, where I was on my return from Washington, and found my army between Middletown and Newton, having been driven back about four miles. I here took the affair in hand, and quickly marched the corps forward, formed a compact line of battle to repulse an attack of the enemy, which was done handsomely at about one o'clock P.M. At three P.M., after some changes of the cavalry from the left to the right flank, I attacked with great vigor, driving and routing the enemy, capturing, according to the last report, forty-three pieces of artillery, and very many prisoners. I have to regret the loss of General Bidwell, killed, and Generals Wright, Grover, and Ricketts, wounded. Wright is slightly wounded. Affairs at times looked badly, but, by the gallantry of our brave officers and men, disaster has been converted into a splendid victory. Darkness again intervened to shut off greater results. I now occupy Strasburg. As soon as practicable I will send you further particulars.

[Signed.]

P. H. SHERIDAN,
Major-General.

INDEX OF AUTHORS.

INDEX OF FIRST LINES.

University Press: John Wilson and Son, Cambridge.

MESSRS. ROBERTS BROTHERS'
Classic Series.

———◆———

A collection of world-renowned works selected from the literatures of all nations, printed from new type in the best manner, and neatly and durably bound. Handy books, convenient to hold, and an ornament to the library shelves.

READY AND IN PREPARATION.

SIR WALTER SCOTT'S "LAY OF THE LAST MINSTREL," "MARMION," and "THE LADY OF THE LAKE." The three poems in one volume.

"There are no books for boys like these poems by Sir Walter Scott. Every boy likes them, if they are not put into his hands too late. *They surpass everything for boy reading.*" — *Ralph Waldo Emerson.*

OLIVER GOLDSMITH'S "THE VICAR OF WAKEFIELD." With Illustrations by Mulready.

DEFOE'S "ROBINSON CRUSOE." With Illustrations by Stothard.

BERNARDIN DE SAINT-PIERRE'S "PAUL AND VIRGINIA." With Illustrations by Lalauze.

SOUTHEY'S "LIFE OF NELSON." With Illustrations by Birket Foster.

VOLTAIRE'S "LIFE OF CHARLES THE TWELFTH." With Maps and Portraits.

MARIA EDGEWORTH'S "CLASSIC TALES." With a biographical Sketch by Grace A. Oliver.

LORD MACAULAY'S "LAYS OF ANCIENT ROME." With a Biographical Sketch and Illustrations.

BUNYAN'S "PILGRIM'S PROGRESS." With all of the original Illustrations in fac-simile.

CLASSIC HEROIC BALLADS. Edited by the Editor of "Quiet Hours."

CLASSIC TALES. By Anna Letitia Barbauld. With a Biographical Sketch by Grace A. Oliver.

CLASSIC TALES. By Ann and Jane Taylor. With a Biographical Sketch by Grace A. Oliver.

AND OTHERS.

THE "WISDOM SERIES." Edited by the editor of "Quiet Hours" and "Sursum Corda." 16mo. Cloth, red edges. Flexible covers. Price per vol., . . . $ .50
Selections from the Imitation of Christ, by Thomas à Kempis; Selections from the Thoughts of Marcus Aurelius Antoninus; Sunshine in the Soul (poems selected by the editor of "Quiet Hours"), First Series; Sunshine in the Soul, Second Series; Selections from Epictetus; The Wisdom of Jesus, the Son of Sirach: or Ecclesiasticus; The Wisdom of Solomon, and other Selections from the Apocrypha; Selections from Fénelon; The Life and Sermons of the Rev. Doctor John Tauler; Socrates, the Apology and Crito of Plato; Socrates, the Phædo of Plato. The above are also published in six volumes complete, enclosed in a handsome box, and include everything issued thus far. Price for the set, ... $4.50

"The editor who gave us the excellent volume of selected poems called 'Quiet Hours,' and who has just prepared another and similar book, has done the public a service by here putting together in compact form the best of the thoughts and aspirations which this generation is too little disposed to look for amidst the less pregnant and valuable matter with which they are mingled in the full editions. A brief but compact and readable memoir prefaces each volume." — *Unitarian Review.*

SUNSHINE IN THE SOUL. Poems selected by the editor of "Quiet Hours." Second Series, uniform with the First Series. 18mo. Cloth, red edges. Price, . . $ .50
The two series in one volume. Cloth, red edges. Price, .75

"The compiler of 'Quiet Hours,' and other volumes of hymns and serious poems, has made a second collection of the poems that are so soothing, helpful and encouraging that she calls them 'Sunshine in the Soul.' They are published in the 'Wisdom Series' of Roberts Brothers, and can be carried about in one's pocket until they are transferred to one's memory, and have done their work of bringing light into dark places."

"Although it is small enough to fit easily in either a lady's or gentleman's pocket, it contains about one hundred and fifteen poems carefully selected from the popular and standard writers. In turning over the delicate little pages we see the names of Longfellow over 'The Legend Beautiful' and 'To-morrow,' and Christina G. Rosetti's over 'Who Shall Deliver Me?' There is also Whittier's name, Miss Mulock's, Wordsworth's, Faber's, Susan Coolidge's and many others, who have written tenderly, sweetly or helpfully upon higher or better thoughts of life, death and the world to come." — *School Journal.*

₊ Our publications are for sale by all booksellers, or will be sent post-paid on receipt of advertised price.

ROBERTS BROTHERS, Boston.

GEORGE SAND. Famous Women Series. By BERTHA THOMAS. One volume. 16mo. Cloth. Price, . . $1.00

"The volume before us, which is published in the series of brief biographies of famous women, of which we have upon previous occasions taken favorable notice, will give its readers a clear and generally adequate idea of George Sand's character and genius, and will serve to correct many misconceptions in regard to the nature of her writings which ignorance and prejudice have spread abroad. At the same time Miss Thomas has sought rather to portray the character of the famous French woman to whom she pays tribute than to criticise or expound the long line of novels which her fertile imagination produced. Her book is rather biographical than literary in its purpose and inspiration, and though the Sand romances are reviewed, and their distinctive characteristics appreciatively and intelligently described, the volume depends for its value and interest upon its narrative and portraiture. It is pleasantly, gracefully and cleverly written, and will worthily sustain the already high reputation of the series to which it belongs." — *North American, Phila.*

"The best of the biography is that we gain from it good, definite notions of the early home, the convent, the marriage with M. Dudevant and how it came about, the short family life, and the circumstances of the early residence in Paris. Each change down to the last scenes of George Sand's life is characterized. So also are the books, which are classified and briefly described. So is that wonderful mental life, so flaming, so easily working itself into words and deeds, so much less removed in subtlety from our common life of common people than was the mental life of almost any other great genius. Owing to the sound and practical treatment which the subject receives at Miss Thomas' hands, the book is plain, readable, adapted to the widest circle of readers, doing in no respect injustice to the mighty soul whose course Miss Thomas can trace and describe, but not as one could who had taken the same flights, or others as high, if not the same. The Famous Women series is a notable one.— *Boston Courier.*

TEN TIMES ONE IS TEN. The Possible Reformation. By E. E. HALE. One volume. 16mo. Cloth. Price, . $1.00

"Notwithstanding the assertion of the title-page, the Rev. E. E. Hale is the author of the story under notice, and it is marked by all the well-known characteristics of his peculiar style. It is an account of a remarkable movement which had for its object the amelioration of human existence by carrying out those principles of a truism which Auguste Comte is credited with having formulated, but which were first embodied in the teachings of Christianity, and which find in the golden rule their tersest and highest expression. Mr. Hale is an interesting writer and a very sympathetic one. He possesses in unusual measure the merit of naturalness. He is a true realist, but instead of placing before his readers the sins, crimes and weaknesses of men, he presents only those things which are honest and of good report. The impression made by such books as his is wholly good. They tend to make their readers better and happier and more useful in their social and civil relations, and we hope that 'Ten Times One is Ten' will have a wide circulation." — *North American, Phila.*

"Roberts Brothers have issued a new edition of 'Ten Times One is Ten,' by Edward Everett Hale, one of the cleverest of our writers. It is a racy little book, inculcating wholesome morals in an effective and almost captivating way. It is worth a score of the average Sunday-school books, and has a habit of getting itself read by whoever takes it up." — *New York Star.*

*** Our publications are for sale by all booksellers, or will be sent post-paid on receipt of advertised price.

ROBERTS BROTHERS, Boston.

THE NO NAME NOVELS.

"No one of the numerous series of novels, with which the country has been deluged of late, contains as many good volumes of fiction as the 'No Name,'" says *Scribner's Monthly.*

FIRST SERIES.—Mercy Philbrick's Choice; Afterglow; Deirdrè; Hetty's Strange History; Is That All? Will Denbigh, Nobleman; Kismet; The Wolf at the Door; The Great Match; Marmorne; Mirage; A Modern Mephistopheles; Gemini; A Masque of Poets. 14 vols. Black and gold.

SECOND SERIES.—Signor Monaldini's Niece; The Colonel's Opera Cloak; His Majesty, Myself; Mrs. Beauchamp Brown; Salvage; Don John; The Tsar's Window; Manuela Parédes; Baby Rue; My Wife and My Wife's Sister; Her Picture; Aschenbroedel. 12 vols. Green and gold.

THIRD SERIES.—The publishers, flattered with the reception given to the First and Second Series of "No Name Novels," among which may be named several already famous in the annals of fiction, will continue the issue with a Third Series, which will retain the original features of the First and Second Series, but in a new style of binding. Already published: Her Crime; Little Sister; Barrington's Fate; A Daughter of the Philistines; Princess Amélie. Price per vol., . $1.00

New Editions of Popular Poets.

JEAN INGELOW'S POETICAL WORKS. With portrait. The only complete edition, and the only edition published with her sanction. Household edition, with red-line border, gilt edges. Cloth, black and gold. Price, $1.25

"I greatly wish that Messrs. ROBERTS BROTHERS might have the exclusive right to publish my books in America. I consider that enlightened nations, as well as individuals, ought to recognize the right of authors, both to power over and to property in their works."—JEAN INGELOW.

CHRISTINA G. ROSSETTI'S POETICAL WORKS. With portrait. Household edition, with red-line border, gilt edges. Cloth, black and gold. Price, . . . $2.00

DANTE GABRIEL ROSSETTI'S POETICAL WORKS. With portrait. Household edition, with red-line border, gilt edges. Cloth, black and gold. Price, . . . $2.00

JOAQUIN MILLER'S POETICAL WORKS. With portrait. Household edition, with red-line border, gilt edges. Cloth, black and gold. Price, . . . $2.00

EDWIN ARNOLD'S POETICAL WORKS. (Including "The Light of Asia.") Household edition, with red-line border, gilt edges. Cloth, black and gold. Price, . $2.00

JOHN KEATS' POETICAL WORKS. Lord Houghton's edition, with a Memoir. With portrait. Household edition, with red-line border, gilt edges. Cloth, black and gold. Price, ... $2.00

* Our publications are for sale by all booksellers, or will be sent post-paid on receipt of advertised price.

ROBERTS BROTHERS, Boston.

GATHERINGS FROM AN ARTIST'S PORTFOLIO IN ROME. By JAMES E. FREEMAN. The author, an American artist, long resident in Rome, gives an entertaining account of life in Rome, with reminiscences and tales, as the result of his personal experience. 12mo. Cloth. Price, ... $1.50

"It is in some respects a sequel to a very interesting volume from the same hand, which appeared three years ago under a similar title. It is an uncommonly bright, attractive and well-written book, pleasingly natural in style, full of information gracefully conveyed, picturesque in its descriptive portions, and overflowing with spirited sketches of character and events. In addition, the book has a touch of refined Bohemianism that lends it a special charm. The work is one that will be perused with genuine pleasure by readers of cultivated tastes." — *Saturday Evening Gazette.*

PLISH AND PLUM. From the German of William Busch, author of "Max Maurice." By CHARLES T. BROOKS. With 100 illustrations. 12mo. Cloth. Price, . . $1.00

"Roberts Brothers, Boston, have published in 'Plish and Plum' one of the most delightful juveniles imaginable. It is translated from the German of William Busch by Chas. T. Brooks, and is the history of two uncommonly lively and rascally dogs. Plish is a slender and demure fellow, Plum a fat, smirking young wretch — both have an equally diabolical power of mischief. Their puppyhood is a time of woe to their possessors, the little Peter and Paul, who repeat in person and character the traits of their pets. How a comfortable dose of birch corrects and improves the four, and how the reward of virtue is bestowed upon them, must be left to the enraptured youngster to find out. The many illustrations, which more than the text tell the story, are little more than outlines, but are so humorous that they would almost bring a laugh to the lips of a graven image. There are such merriment, freshness and healthfulness about the little book, that the boy who gets it in his stocking is blest indeed." — *Tribune.*

New Editions of the Following Popular Books:

NONSENSE SONGS, Stories, Botany and Alphabets. By EDWARD LEAR. With colored illustrations. Square 12mo. Half cloth, illuminated covers. Price, . . . $1.25

MAX AND MAURICE: A Juvenile History in Seven Books. By WILLIAM BUSCH. With colored illustrations. 12mo. Half cloth, illuminated covers. Price, . . $ .75

POSIES FOR CHILDREN. A Book of Verse. Selected by Mrs. A. C. LOWELL. With illustrations. Small quarto. Illuminated cloth. Price, ... $1.50

OLD-FASHIONED FAIRY TALES. The original Munroe and Francis edition. Fully illustrated. Complete in one volume. Square 16mo. Red and black lettered. Price, ... $1.50

⁂ Our publications are for sale by all booksellers, or will be sent post-paid on receipt of advertised price.

ROBERTS BROTHERS, Boston.